"Any head back?" Angie asked.

"I have a therapy visit to do with Peppy this afternoon, but I need a quick bite to eat."

"Sure thing. Where do you have in mind?"

"There's a diner..." She told Luke where.

"And where are you visiting after that?"

"An assisted-living place."

"Can I come with you?"

Angie was shocked that he was interested. "I mean, if you want to," she said, studying him, trying to understand his motivations.

"I'd like to get a better idea of what therapy dogs do," Luke said. "Plus, it's a nice day and I'm enjoying being with you."

Angie looked at him, startled, and their gazes held for a second too long. What on earth? He sounded like... Wow. Like he was flirting. Maybe he'd thought her invitation to lunch opened that door?

If Luke was interested in her—the thought flattered and excited her—she had to shut it down. She couldn't be with a man like him.

It would only lead to heartbreak when he learned about her past...

Lee Tobin McClain is the *New York Times* bestselling author of emotional small-town romances featuring flawed characters who find healing through friendship, faith and family. Lee grew up in Ohio and now lives in Western Pennsylvania, where she enjoys hiking with her goofy goldendoodle, visiting writer friends and admiring her daughter's mastery of the latest TikTok dances. Learn more about her books at www.leetobinmcclain.com.

Books by Lee Tobin McClain

Love Inspired

K-9 Companions

Rescue Haven

Redemption Ranch

Visit the Author Profile page at LoveInspired.com for more titles.

HOLDING ONTO SECRETS

LEE TOBIN McCLAIN

LOVE INSPIRED
INSPIRATIONAL ROMANCE

LOVE INSPIRED®
INSPIRATIONAL ROMANCE

ISBN-13: 978-1-335-93726-1

Holding Onto Secrets

Recycling programs
for this product may
not exist in your area.

Love Inspired
22 Adelaide St. West, 41st Floor
Toronto, Ontario M5H 4E3, Canada
www.LoveInspired.com

Printed in Lithuania

MIX
Paper | Supporting
responsible forestry
FSC® C021394

For God shall bring every work into judgment,
with every secret thing, whether it be good,
or whether it be evil.
—*Ecclesiastes* 12:14

To Phoebe,
the sweetest Cavalier King Charles spaniel ever,
and her loving servants, Debbie and Don

Chapter One

Luke Johnson was removing the spray arm from a customer's state-of-the-art dishwasher when he heard a sharp "yip" from the next room.

It broke through the well-modulated women's voices, making several of the wealthy ladies laugh. It made Luke smile, too. He liked animals and would've had a pet if he didn't work ridiculously long hours.

"Does your grandma have a dog?" he asked Caleb, Mrs. Ralston-Jones's eight-year-old grandson, who had been watching Luke's work with interest. Luke was surprised that Mrs. Ralston-Jones, who was very particular about her home, surroundings and image, would have a dog and would allow it to be present at her women's group meeting.

Before the boy could answer, Mrs. Ralston-Jones called from the next room. "Caleb! Come in here, please!"

Caleb groaned.

"You'd better go see what she wants." Luke flashed him a smile. Cute kid. About the same age as Luke's nephew.

Caleb wrinkled his freckled nose. "She's gonna yell at me."

"Caleb! Now, please!" The woman had the voice of a drill sergeant.

Instead of complying, Caleb dove beneath the polished-oak kitchen table.

Uh-oh.

Not my circus, not my monkeys. Luke needed to focus on getting his work done quickly and well. That was how he'd earn enough money to help his sister get past her problems and back to the land of the living. A good handyman was basically invisible to the families he worked for, especially in a wealthy community like this one.

He leaned into the dishwasher and removed the filter. Yuck. Like many other homes in this neighborhood of Chesapeake Corners, Maryland, Mrs. Ralston-Jones's place was mostly pristine. But who let their dishwasher trap get this full of gunk?

He knew the answer: Lots of people. He should be grateful. It was just one of the many neglected home maintenance chores that kept a handyman like him busy six and sometimes seven days per week.

He moved to the sink and focused on cleaning the filter, not on the click-click-click of heels as Mrs. Ralston-Jones stomped into the room. She tugged Caleb from his hiding place. "I said to come," the woman hissed, "and your disobedience is embarrassing." She led the protesting child out of the kitchen.

Then Caleb squealed with excitement. Another yip.

"You may play with the dog after you read to the ladies," Mrs. Ralston-Jones said, her voice carrying loud and clear from the next room. "Sit down right here."

"Aw, Grandma…"

"Read. Now. Here's your book."

"No, Grandma, please!"

"Buck up, boy!" Mrs. Ralston-Jones's voice now sounded even more irritated. "You can read this story. It's meant for toddlers!"

"Forget about us ladies, honey," another woman said. Her voice was low, husky, sweet. "Just read to the dog."

Luke went still, turned off the water and listened. That voice was so familiar…

"Bob…has…a…c-c-cat…" Long pause and then the sound of a book being thrown to the floor. "I can't."

Fortunately, the answering chorus of ladies' voices sounded gentle. "It's okay" and "Reading is hard" and "You can try again."

Luke was fitting the filter back into the dishwasher when that memorable voice sounded again. "Maybe if we let Caleb read to the dog in a different room, without an audience—"

"He just needs to work harder!" Mrs. Ralston-Jones interrupted.

Luke wiped sweat from his forehead, and it wasn't related to the mid-May Maryland heat. It was her, the woman with the familiar, smoky voice. She'd caught his attention, evoked his pity, nine or maybe ten years ago. He'd never forgotten her.

But then as now, women like that were out of his league.

"Caleb, try again!" Mrs. Ralston-Jones ordered.

Running footsteps came back into the kitchen. This time, the kid hid behind Luke.

That was hard to ignore, but Luke tried. He was just the handyman, working extra hours now to finance the residential treatment program his sister needed.

He had to pretend he didn't see the drama. To make nice with the customer, for his sister's sake.

More clicking heels. "You *will* get out here and read to the ladies!"

"I don't want to, Grandma!" Caleb sounded desperate.

The woman approached, her hand out like a claw. The kid scooted under the open dishwasher door.

Mrs. Ralston-Jones continued scolding and reaching for Caleb.

A smart guy would pretend he had to get something in his truck, escape this situation, leave this overprivileged family to work out their own issues. But he couldn't help but empathize with a boy the same age as his nephew. If someone were attacking Declan, no way would Luke let it go.

Luke sighed, stood and stepped between Mrs. Ralston-Jones and the child. He was a good foot taller than Mrs. Ralston-Jones. "Look," he said, "putting on the pressure isn't going to help a kid who's having a hard time."

Mrs. Ralston-Jones looked startled that Luke had addressed her. "And what authority do you have?"

Luke lifted a shoulder, still blocking her from the boy. "I was a struggling kid myself." Reading had been tough for him, until his foster mom and the school had realized he had dyslexia. He still remembered the dread that had clutched his stomach every time his turn to read aloud approached, still remembered the laughter of the other children.

"Yes, well, look at you now. I want more for my grandson."

Luke blew out a breath, looking away. *Don't react. This is about a kid, not you.*

"Priscilla." The low, sultry voice he'd noticed before stilled Luke, calmed him. "I may have a solution."

Standing in the doorway was a woman with long red hair and an incredibly beautiful face who looked...yes. It was her. She'd probably been in her midtwenties when he'd seen her before, but although ten years had passed, she didn't look a day older.

Scratch that. Her green eyes revealed a depth of experience you didn't have in your twenties.

"Everyone has a solution today," Mrs. Ralston-Jones snapped.

Luke couldn't take his eyes off the woman in the doorway. Flame-red hair rippling down almost to her waist, big green eyes, pink cheeks that betrayed her agitation with the scene in front of her.

She was the most gorgeous woman he'd ever seen. Wealthy too, but boy, he didn't envy her. Being married to a cheater topped his list of bad life situations.

Anyway, women like her were out of reach for a guy like him.

He was fine with that.

Mrs. Ralston-Jones leaned around Luke and saw the feet sticking out from beneath the dishwasher door. "Caleb! Come out now!"

"The Reading to Dogs program might work better in a library or school setting," the woman said. Her voice was gentle, but Luke heard the edge in it.

Mrs. Ralston-Jones waved the beautiful woman's words away.

"Children who are learning need a lot of practice," the woman went on, still in that amazing voice. "But reading to teachers, or even to other kids, makes them anxious. Then it's hard for them to think and remember. Reading to an animal—without an audience—gives them practice without the pressure."

A small brown-and-white dog trotted into the room, tail wagging.

Caleb shimmied out from beneath the dishwasher door. "Can I play with her?"

"No!" The grandmother reached for him, nearly tripping over the little dog.

Luke sidestepped, blocking her outstretched arm with his hand. It gave the kid a head start as he bolted off.

The grandmother's mouth opened in an angry, lipsticked

O. "How dare you prevent me from taking control of my grandson!"

"Uh, sorry, but the kid seems to be having a rough day."

The red-haired woman picked up the dog. Luke hoped she would leave, because she was distracting him, but instead she leaned against the door jamb, watching.

From the next room, the murmur of women's voices continued. Women could talk through anything, it seemed.

"I don't appreciate your interference," Mrs. Ralston-Jones was saying, glaring at Luke. "You can leave. Now."

Great. *Stay calm.* "I'd like to do some cleanup after I've finished with the dishwasher."

She looked down her nose at the appliance. "The maid will take care of it."

He sighed. The maid was his sister. "She's not able to come in today."

"Why not?"

He shifted from one foot to the other, crinkling the paper covers over his work boots. "It's a health issue," he said.

"Again?" Mrs. Ralston-Jones propped her hands on her hips. "Look, there are other, more cooperative families in this area who need the work. As of this moment, you and your sister are both fired."

Luke blew out a sigh and avoided the eyes of the beautiful woman. He needed the work a mansion-owning woman like Mrs. Ralston-Jones could provide to a handyman. And even with his own contribution, his sister needed to work as much as she was able to. He forced himself to grovel. "I'm sorry, ma'am. I hope you'll reconsider. For now, I'll clean up and get out of your hair."

"See that you do." She strode out of the room. The beautiful woman shot him a sympathetic glance and then followed, the dog in her arms.

Out the window, he saw Caleb running through the grass in the sizeable backyard. The boy reached an apple tree and shimmied up with obvious skill.

Good. At least someone was having a better day than he was.

Angie Anderson straightened her spine and managed a cheery goodbye wave to the small group of women in Mrs. Ralston-Jones's living room. Then she followed her hostess to the front door. "Thank you for taking the time to meet with me," she said. "I hope you find a charity to support that fits your needs better."

The older woman huffed. "I know you lost your husband, and Oscar was a wonderful man, but it's been almost two years. You can't play the sympathy card forever."

"Play the..." *Wow.* Angie knew Mrs. Ralston-Jones's rudeness was tolerated because she was by far the wealthiest woman in town. Angie had never been on the receiving end of the rudeness, though. Probably protected by her late husband's position, reputation and wealth.

That protection was gone now. Angie wasn't in dire straits financially, but she couldn't fund her entire therapy-dog program herself, especially since Oscar's estate was taking such a long time to settle. She needed donors for the project that was so close to her heart.

Obviously, she wasn't going to find them here.

She forced a smile and hurried toward her car, juggling her purse, a bin of display materials she hadn't gotten the opportunity to use, and Peppy.

The handyman she'd seen before was loading supplies into his pickup truck. Hmmm. She set her things in her car and approached him, holding Peppy's leash. "Hello, sir?"

He turned, a strange expression on his face. "Hi, there."

"Um, I couldn't help overhearing Priscilla let you go," she said. "If it makes you feel any better, I'm out on my ear, too."

"Oh?" He slammed his tailgate closed.

"Yeah. She doesn't want her group to contribute to my dog reading program." Why was he looking at her that way?

"Too bad." He leaned back against his truck and crossed his very muscular arms. There was some gray in his beard, she could see now, and some fine lines fanning out from his brown eyes. So he wasn't as young as she'd initially thought. Late thirties, most likely.

"Yeah. So, anyway, I wondered if you're available to do some—"

"Hey, lady!" Mrs. Ralston-Jones's grandson ran up to them. Poor kid, he'd been so embarrassed when he couldn't read well on command, but he seemed to have recovered. He stopped and knelt beside Peppy, petting her gently. "Did you mean it about reading to your dog? I like dogs."

She smiled at him. "Yes, I did mean it."

"When?"

"Soon." She needed funding for the overall program, but she already did therapy work with Peppy. "Who's your teacher? I can see if we can arrange a classroom visit."

Caleb waved a hand. "Second grade's almost over. But I hafta go to summer school. You could bring Peppy there."

"We'll see," she said. He was so cute. She'd always wanted kids, but it hadn't been in God's plan for her, it seemed.

An SUV pulled up in the driveway. "That's my mom," Caleb said. "I gotta go." With one last scratch of Peppy's soft ears, he ran toward the other vehicle.

"Cute kid," the handyman said. They both watched the SUV pull away.

"He is." She bit her lip. "Like I was saying before, I need some work done. Do you have any openings?"

He tilted his head to one side. "Doesn't your husband usually arrange for work on your house?"

What on earth? "It's the twenty-first century. I actually make my own arrangements."

"Oh! I didn't mean you couldn't…it's just…" He lifted his hands, palms up. "Sorry. My schedule's tight this week, but since I was planning to spend the rest of the morning here, I could come take a look." He reached into his pocket and handed her a business card. "Or you can give me a call."

"Now works, if you want to follow me to my place," she said.

"Sure thing." He started to climb into his truck, then leaned back out. "By the way," he said, "I remember you."

Chapter Two

It was never a good thing when a man said, "I remember you."

Angie got out of her car and took deep breaths, the sight of her Craftsman-style cottage, with its surrounding trees and narrow, rushing stream, helping her effort to get calm.

Luke Johnson didn't seem like the kind of guy who would have visited her past workplace. But one thing she'd learned about men: there was no predicting what went on inside their heads, or what bad habits they might have.

At any rate, she wasn't going to judge. Had no room to do so. She waited while he got out of his truck and approached.

"Nice place," he said. "I thought you lived over near where Mrs. Ralston-Jones lives."

"Used to," she said, studying him. The house where she'd lived with Oscar had felt way too big and formal once he'd passed away, and she'd never regretted moving to this smaller place. "Why?"

"I think I did some work for your husband, way back," he said. "That's why I thought…anyway. Tell me what you're looking for here."

She led him behind the cottage and to the wooded area at the end of the long backyard. "I'm thinking of building a small kennel and dog run over here," she said. "It'll allow me to take in some rescue dogs and test them out for therapy work."

He studied the landscape, nodding. "That's doable," he said. "What's that building over there?"

"Just an old shed," she said. "I'm scared to look inside, to be honest. It has a hole in the wall, and who knows what critters have made their home there. We'll need to pull it down, most likely." The shed was actually cute, shaped like a small barn, painted red. But Angie was a wimp about bugs and bats and rodents.

"Let's take a look." He led the way through the knee-high grass, stomping it down with his work boots as he went. She followed, picking her way more gingerly. She should have put on sneakers, but she hadn't known he'd want to explore.

"Mind if I open it up and look inside?"

"Be my guest. I'm staying back."

"Chicken." He flashed her a smile and opened the door.

Something whooshed out, and she ducked, letting out an undignified squeal.

He backed out, laughing. "There's a family of starlings inside, and most likely a few mice. But at a glance, it seems structurally sound aside from the hole in the wall, which could be fixed. What do you think of using the shed somehow in your plans?"

"I guess we could." Hesitantly, she made her way forward and peeked inside. A few rusty pieces of yard equipment were heaped in one corner, and the dust made her cough, but it wasn't nearly as bad as she'd expected.

Peppy pulled on her leash, and she let the dog come forward, where she poked her nose into several corners. She jumped back when something skittered across the floor.

Luke grinned. "Not a hunting dog, I guess."

"No." She laughed and led Peppy out of the shed. "She's a lover, not a fighter."

"She's sure cute." Luke knelt and rubbed Peppy's head and

ears, and the dog looked up at him, her big brown eyes adoring. "Soft, too. I can see why she'd be a good therapy dog."

"Yeah. She's great visiting nursing homes and hospitals, but she really shines with kids." She studied the shed and the area around it, frowning. "If we could use the shed and create the dog run more economically, then I might be able to get a start on renovating my carriage house, too."

"Let's take a look," he said easily, and she led him back across the yard. Peppy, now off leash, ran ahead toward the house.

"So how come you're doing all this work with kids and dogs?" He was shortening his strides to match hers. "If you don't mind my asking."

She glanced sideways at him. There was no judgment in his expression, and he'd said he thought he'd done work for her and her husband in the past. In their big home, they'd had a lot of different contractors and workers in. She didn't remember them all.

If he knew her from that part of the past, that was better than him knowing her from before.

"I want to do something purposeful, now that my husband's gone," she said. "Books and dogs were what saved me, and I'd like to pass that on to others."

"Saved you, huh?" He lifted an eyebrow, but didn't comment further, and she didn't elaborate.

She also didn't share her other reason: that she wasn't ever going to have kids. She'd wanted them, badly. But her husband hadn't, and she hadn't felt she had the leverage to push him in a direction he didn't want to go. She was just so grateful to him for rescuing her from the cesspool she'd been swimming in when they'd met.

She led the way over to the garage. "It's got living space up above. I'm thinking of fixing it up to rent it out, but that's probably not on the table yet." She met his eyes. "I can pay the going rate for your services, but funds aren't unlimited. I'm not sure when I can fit this into the budget."

He looked thoughtful. "Can I take a look at the structure?"

"Sure," she said, shrugging. She started to open the garage door, but he beat her to it and lifted it effortlessly. They both walked inside, and he was quiet as he walked up the stairs and poked around the area.

When he came down, his head was tilted to one side. "If you're interested," he said, "I'd like to propose an exchange."

As soon as the words were out of Luke's mouth, he regretted them. He already found Angie way too attractive. He needed to increase the distance between them, not draw closer. A woman like Angie was not for him.

"What sort of exchange?" she asked.

"Never mind," he said quickly. "Foolish idea."

"Tell me." She gave him an encouraging smile that made his heart melt a little.

He looked toward the upper floor of the carriage house, giving himself a chance to stop fixating on her beauty. "It wouldn't work. I was thinking I…" He stopped. Even telling her the idea would be admitting his need for a place to live, his poverty compared to her financial situation.

She waited, not rushing him, but not filling in the silence, either.

Just say it. It didn't matter whether or not she respected him or scorned him. It didn't matter that she didn't seem to remember him. "I'm looking for an inexpensive place to live," he said. "The apartment I rented when I moved back to town isn't worth the price, and my lease is up at the end of May."

Instead of looking surprised or scornful, she wrinkled

her nose and nodded. "It can be tough finding an affordable place to live. I've been there."

That was hard to believe. "I was thinking that it wouldn't take much to make your carriage house livable. I could clean it up a little, move in and work on the renovation nights after I'm done with my regular jobs."

"Really?" She sounded doubtful.

"Like I said, silly idea. You probably don't want someone living on your property, anyway."

"Actually," she said, "I do. As soon as I saw this property, I figured I could rent out the garage apartment. It's just I wasn't thinking to put that project at the top of the list. But let's take a look." She was off, trotting up the stairs before he could stop her.

What could he do but follow?

She was looking around, and he did, too. The main room was musty and dusty, with piles of boards and some old-looking furniture.

He walked into the small kitchen and turned on the water. It sputtered for a moment and then came out clear. He flicked a light switch, and that worked, too.

"Ugh," she said, looking around. "It's a real mess. I should have cleaned it up before, but like I said…not at the top of the list."

Luke thought of where he'd lived in his early years, back when his dad had been trying to provide a home for him and his sister. Compared to some of those places, this was the Taj Mahal. "It's got potential," he said. "Mostly just needs to be cleaned up. You can remodel it at some point, but it would work fine for a single guy. Only…" He trailed off and blew out a sigh.

"What?"

He might as well tell her the deal-breaker now. "It may

not just be for me, or not entirely. I have my nephew stay with me sometimes. He's eight."

She lifted her hands and wrinkled her nose again, which made her look like a young girl. "I have no problem with kids—I like them. But there's just one bedroom. It's pretty small for a kid."

Obviously, she had no idea of poverty. "There's a great yard and there will be dogs. Believe me, it'll be a step up for him." Any place would be, considering the run-down house his sister lived in.

"I see your point," she said, surprising him. "And I'd end up with an apartment I could rent out, eventually."

"Right." He scanned the place, thinking. Then he walked over to the window and looked outside, tilting his head to avoid hitting the slanted ceiling. "It would probably take a week or ten days to get your outdoor projects started, given that I have other jobs lined up. Depending on what you want, those could be finished in a month or six weeks. I could work on this place a little at a time, in the evenings."

"You like working a lot?" She looked suddenly pensive. "My late husband did. Worked all the time."

Luke bit his tongue to keep back the response that wanted to come out: her husband hadn't been working all the time he said he was. But she probably knew it, probably hated the man. "That must have been hard on you," he said finally.

"Hard on me?" She looked at him blankly. "Hey, a man who has a job and earns a living was a big step up for me, and Oscar was a good guy."

No, he wasn't. But Luke definitely wouldn't say anything about what he'd seen, especially if Angie still held on to her illusions about the man. No reason to speak ill of the dead. "So, if I did the work on this place for you, what do you think you'd charge for rent?"

"I'd pay you the rate we discussed for my other projects," she said. "If you really want to do the work on this place, you could live here rent free."

"That doesn't seem fair."

"Why not? I wouldn't have been using it, anyway. And it means I have my handyman close by if something goes wrong."

"I can't turn that down." He held out a hand. "If you mean it, we have a deal."

"Deal," she said, putting her hand into his.

It felt small and delicate and just plain good, so he dropped it after a quick shake.

Angie was sweet as well as beautiful, but she seemed naïve. Letting a guy she'd basically just met come to live on her property, rent free?

He'd make sure to give her work equivalent to the amount of rent he should have paid. Unlike her late husband, *he* wasn't going to take advantage.

And he also wasn't going to get closer to her. They were from different worlds. She needed him now, for his skills, but that was the only reason she was being nice to him. People like her didn't like people like him for themselves.

Which was fine. He just had to keep his head down and do his job. Get his sister into her program and make sure his nephew was okay and earn some extra money.

"I'll stop by when I can and do some cleaning," he said. "If it's all right with you, I'll move in Saturday. I don't have a lot of stuff." He did have a lot of baggage, of the emotional kind, but she didn't need to know about that.

God had put this opportunity into his life, and he'd embrace it. What he *wouldn't* embrace was the woman in front of him, smiling and smelling like the May flowers that bloomed outside her cottage.

Chapter Three

On Tuesday afternoon, Angie watched Caleb read to Peppy in the school library. From a distance, because that was the best way to do reading-to-dogs therapy: adults stayed out of it.

Caleb read slowly, his finger running along the page, stopping often to pet and cuddle with Peppy. That was fine, too. For a struggling reader to feel happy with a book in his hands was a huge step.

A few older kids worked on projects in the school library, surrounded by books and computers. One boy jumped up and rushed to a globe, spinning it around until he found what he was looking for, then beckoning to the girl he'd been working with.

Rain dripped down the windows that lined one wall, making tracks and obscuring the view of the Chesapeake Bay outside. The smell of books and sweaty kids and the sound of the librarian's computer keys clicking, all of it made Angie both happy and sad.

She watched a mom volunteer shelving books. That was what she'd longed for, once she'd gotten safe and settled in with Oscar: the chance to be a mom and raise a child. She'd definitely have been the mom who volunteered in the school library. But Oscar had said, understandably, that he was too old to start a family. She hadn't been in a position to argue her point, not when he'd given her so much.

Maybe working with kids was what God had in mind for her. She could enjoy them and help them, even if she didn't take them home at night.

"Five more minutes, Caleb," the librarian called.

"Aw, no!"

"Yes. Finish up." The librarian smiled at Angie. "Believe me, that's the first time Caleb has wanted to linger in the library. It's a terrific thing you're doing. I hope you'll come back often."

"I hope so, too."

She was glad to be distracted from the big changes she'd just introduced into her life. Namely, Luke Johnson. He'd stopped by yesterday evening and started carrying junk out of her carriage house. She'd been busy hosting a small group of neighbors, but she'd taken a couple of glances at him out the window. Her guests had left just as it was getting dark, and so had Luke, but he hadn't taken the opportunity to come talk. He'd just waved and climbed into his truck.

And that was good. Luke was not for her. He was simply doing work on her house and property, and he was going to help her get her therapy reading dog program up and growing. That was what was important.

When the warning bell rang, she picked up Peppy and walked with Caleb back to the classroom so Peppy could say goodbye to the other children. Several who hadn't gotten to read to Peppy bemoaned the dog's departure.

"I wish I could have read to the dog!" a blond boy said to Caleb.

"You'll get your chance next time, Declan," the teacher said to him, then looked inquiringly at Angie. "You'll come back, won't you? We could use about six of you, to be honest."

"Actually, I'm working on that." As the students packed up, chattering and laughing, she told the teacher, Gabby, about her plans to start a program training therapy dogs and teams.

"That sounds wonderful," Gabby said. "I can't believe I never met you before. Let's stay in touch." She spun and clapped her hands with the multitasking ability that seemed to be a part of most elementary teachers' makeup. "The faster you get into your lines, the faster we can go outside."

The bell rang and the kids rushed to their places, and soon everyone was walking out. Caleb ran over to Angie, and she put Peppy down so Caleb could give the tired dog one last pat.

"Can I pet him, too?" the little boy named Declan, who'd been upset he didn't get a chance to read to Peppy, begged.

"Of course!" Angie walked slowly beside the boys, giving them the chance to be with Peppy while trying not to hinder their progress outside.

The rain had stopped. About half of the kids in Gabby's class climbed onto buses, while the other half lingered in a group near the line of cars. Some parents had parked and gotten out, chatting while their kids ran around, occasionally scolding the kids for jumping and playing in puddles.

A woman got out of her SUV and walked toward the children. Caleb rushed to her. "Mom! I read to the dog! I was good at it!"

Caleb's mother knelt down and hugged him, disregarding the wet pavement. "Good job, kiddo," she said. When Caleb ran back over to the other kids, his mother came to where Angie and Gabby were standing. "Thank you so much for setting up this reading-to-dogs thing," she said to Gabby.

Gabby held out a hand as if she were presenting Angie. "Megan, this is Angie, the one who handles the dogs. She's trying to grow her program, and I think it's great. Angie, meet Megan, Caleb's mom."

Megan turned to Angie and recognition dawned. "Oh, man, you were at my mom's place the other day. I heard she was hard on you, and I'm sorry. I think it's a wonderful program, obviously." She smiled at Angie then at Caleb as he ran shouting with the other boys.

"It's fine. I knew it was a long shot, getting their grant."

"You *should* get it," Megan said. "I'd love to see your program grow. But Mom doesn't listen to my opinion very often."

"Uncle Luke!" The shout from Declan, Caleb's friend, seized Angie's attention. The little boy ran to the truck that was becoming familiar to Angie.

"Wait," she said. "Luke is…oh, yeah. He said something about his nephew being Caleb's age."

"Uh-huh." Gabby looked in Luke's direction. "That's Declan's hot uncle."

"He *is* hot," Megan said, matter-of-factly. And why not? It was the simple truth. "Oh, man," the woman added, "I have to apologize to him for Mom. She was pretty mean to him, from what I heard." She headed across the parking lot.

Someone called Gabby away. As Angie turned toward her car, ignoring the tug that made her want to stop and greet Luke, she heard someone calling, "Hey, Angie!"

Angie turned, and her heart sank as she saw who was coming toward her. Shannon, an acquaintance from her husband's life.

"Are you volunteering in the schools, too?" the woman asked, her gold bracelets jingling as she air-hugged Angie. "That's nice. I'm sorry for your loss, by the way. But I guess you're sitting pretty now."

Angie stepped back. "What do you mean?"

"I mean, you had to expect…what was Oscar, thirty years older than you?"

"Almost." She smiled at the memory of Oscar's weathered face, his warm smile. He'd truly saved her. After her mother had married an abusive, mean man, Angie had run away. When she'd learned how hard things were on the street and how easily a young girl could be taken advantage of, she'd realized she'd made a mistake. But there was no going back.

She'd had a look men liked and a couple of years of dance lessons back in better times. Exotic dancing had been the best of her options, but it wasn't a good one; she'd hated it and come close to hating men.

And then Oscar had come into the club, met her and treated her with kindness. He'd asked if she was happy and offered to help. Soon they'd fallen in love and married.

The fact that he was so much older had been just fine with Angie. She'd needed someone stable and cool-headed. On some level, she'd probably needed a father figure. Marrying him had improved her life by leaps and bounds.

She definitely hadn't thought ahead to becoming a widow and inheriting Oscar's money, or some of it. But people like Shannon would always consider her a gold digger.

She realized that Shannon was still watching her, smirking, eyebrows raised. Peppy, a great judge of character, cowered behind Angie's legs.

"Take care, Shannon," she said and turned away.

And there was Luke, talking with Caleb's mom, Megan. He was laughing at something she was saying, not acting bitter about the way Mrs. Ralston-Jones had treated him.

His smile lit up his face. When Declan ran to him, he swung the boy up in a hug and then instantly put him down before the boy could protest.

Warmth flared inside her, a sense of attraction she'd never felt for anyone before.

"He's a looker," Gabby said, coming up beside her, "but that's a sad situation."

"What's sad?"

"Declan's home life. When Declan's mom is doing poorly, his uncle takes him. She must be having a hard time."

"Is she sick?" Angie was still watching Luke. He'd pulled a football out of his truck and tossed it to Declan, and Caleb and a couple of other children came over to join in the fun.

"Let's just say she struggles," Gabby said, obviously tempted to say more but restraining herself. "She's a nice person, and I like her. But Declan's fortunate to have his uncle. Luke is a strong Christian man, and so kind."

"Declan *is* fortunate. Luke seems like a good guy."

And that was all he could be to her, she reminded herself as she walked to her car with Peppy. A good guy. Because a strong Christian, in particular, couldn't deal with someone from her background. Even if they didn't know the worst of it, they'd probably think like Shannon thought: that Angie was a sleazy person out for an old man's money.

As the children dispersed, Angie drove away, smiling about her momentary attraction to Luke Johnson. She'd felt like a teenager admiring the star quarterback from afar. Maybe she should resist it, but in a way, it was a good sign. It meant she was getting over Oscar's death, coming out from the cloud she'd been living under for almost two years.

Noticing a handsome man probably meant she was healing, but that was all it meant.

Luke cleaned and tightened up Angie's carriage house each evening until Thursday. It was close to ready for him to move in, so he took Thursday evening off to spend time with his sister and do a little work on her house.

It was a warm spring evening. Vanessa lived in a small, run-down house she'd somehow scraped up the money to buy, and Luke hated how shabby it looked. He wasn't going to invest a lot of time into the place, since he hoped to help her find a better home soon, but he could do a little something while he visited. He was painting the trim on her porch while she rocked and sipped a soda and Declan played in the street with some neighborhood kids.

His own apartment was just down the street from Vanessa's house. It was convenient even though the place was a dump, and he dreaded telling Vanessa he was moving across town. Not that the town was huge; the high-income area of Chesapeake Corners, where Angie and Mrs. Ralston-Jones lived, adjoined downtown on one side, and the lower-income area, where he and his sister lived, adjoined it on the other side.

But Vanessa wasn't a big fan of change. He had to tell her tonight.

"You're sure you're okay with having Declan back tonight?" he asked. "I can keep him a couple more days if you need me to." Not that it was easy, fitting in school pickups and finding playdates—which he wasn't allowed to call them, now that Declan was eight—to allow him to work into the evening. Oddly enough, Declan had gone home after school twice with Caleb, Mrs. Ralston-Jones's grandson.

"I'm fine, I'm good. You do way too much for us." Vanessa stretched, her child-size T-shirt riding up her stomach, which was perfectly flat and sported a belly-button ring.

"Did you have dinner?" Luke tried to keep the question casual, offhand.

"Do you want a sandwich? I can make you one."

"Thanks, I already ate." He stopped painting and studied her.

She held up a hand. "I know what you're thinking. I had a protein shake and an apple for dinner."

"That's not—"

"Real food, I know," she interrupted. "I made a pasta bake that Declan can eat for the next few days."

"And you, too."

"Of course." She avoided his eyes and picked up her phone.

Luke went back to his painting, studying his sister in between brush strokes. She had long, wavy blond hair and big eyes. Luke happened to know she was a size two because he'd bought her clothes in the past.

At least, he hoped she was still a size two. To his eye, she looked a little skinnier than she had a few months ago.

His jaw clenched as he focused on his painting. He'd paid his last rent check for a while, and he was making good money during the days. Once he got the carriage house in decent shape, he could start on Angie's dog run and kennel.

If the numbers he'd run in his head were correct, he'd be able to pay for a residential treatment program for Vanessa by the end of the summer. But would it be soon enough?

Vanessa's anorexia had started back when they were teens, and it had ebbed and flowed over the past few years. Motherhood had been a lot for her, and several times she'd drunk too much without eating and fallen. The illness had made her bones brittle, and the last time she'd fallen, she'd broken both wrists. Declan had called Luke in a panic, and he'd rushed over. When he'd found her crying, reeking of alcohol, he'd taken her to the hospital.

Her wrists had healed, and she'd gotten some counseling. But Luke had talked with several doctors and a psychologist who specialized in eating disorders, and he'd learned that residential treatment offered the best chance for success. Since neither Luke nor Vanessa had benefits, the limited insurance he could afford for them didn't cover it.

He looked up and saw that she was picking at her nails, a sure sign of stress. "Hey, Nessie," he said, using his old name for her. "Remember this?" He dabbed paint onto his nose.

As he'd hoped, she cracked up. "Ma Christianson was so mad!" She'd been their favorite and longest-term foster mom, strict but fair. She'd given them the task of painting a shed, and they'd sneaked up on her when she was sleeping and dotted red paint on her nose.

Declan came over to see what they were laughing about, and they told him as Luke wiped the paint off his face. Declan flopped down on the steps, and Vanessa got him a glass of lemonade.

"Guess what, Mom!" Declan said when she returned. He downed the entire glass then spoke again. "This lady brought her dog to school on Tuesday, and some of the kids got to read to the dog. It was so cool! I didn't get to, though. But she might come back."

It was the best lead-in Luke was going to get. "I think it was Miss Angie who brought the dog, right? Little brown-and-white pup? Named Peppy?"

"Yeah! I got to pet her."

Luke cleared his throat. "Angie's starting a therapy-dog program," he told Vanessa, "and she needs some work done at her place."

"You're going to do it?"

He nodded, sucked in a breath and told her about the carriage house. To his surprise, she wasn't upset about his moving, and neither was Declan once he understood that he could visit his uncle and Peppy at the same time.

"When are you moving?" Vanessa asked.

"Saturday, if I can get the cleanup done by then. My rental's up at the end of the month, and I'd like to not pay another month's rent."

"Makes sense," she said. Then: "Is she cute?" she asked in a teasing voice.

"Who?" Luke asked, even though he was pretty sure she meant Angie.

"Yeah!" Declan said at the same time. "She looks like a movie star!"

"What's her last name? Maybe I know her."

It wasn't that big of a town, but Luke was fairly certain his sister moved in different circles than Angie. "Anderson," he said.

A shadow passed over his sister's face. "Anderson. That's a common name. It probably isn't the family I'm thinking of."

"She's a widow," Luke said. "Young, but I think her husband was older. Her place is on Hanover Street, kind of on the edge of town."

"Oh." Vanessa looked uneasy.

"She just moved there a few months ago. She used to live up on Andover Hill, before her husband died."

Vanessa's eyes widened. Declan went inside to get more lemonade. The sun sank lower, painting the sky purple and orange and gold.

Why was Vanessa looking so odd? Was she afraid of losing his help after all? "Declan will be welcome there anytime," he assured her. "And if you're worried about me getting preoccupied with her and her concerns, well, that's not going to happen. We move in different circles." *And she's way, way out of my league.*

"Good," Vanessa said, "because…well, I knew her husband."

"Really? How?" Luke didn't like his own curiosity about what the man had been like. He didn't need to know anything about Angie's past.

"It was…when I was in my bad phase." She looked at him meaningfully.

"When…what do you mean?" His sister's bad phase had involved her making a lot of negative choices, including choices about men. But she couldn't have…

She was watching him. "I knew him pretty well," she said. "Well, actually not, because I didn't know his family situation. But I *knew* him."

Luke's jaw dropped as he realized what she was saying. "You were…involved with him?" He didn't add the question he wanted to ask: *when he was married to Angie?* Was that what his sister had meant when she said she didn't know his family situation? Had he been married, only Vanessa didn't know it?

The sound of crickets rose and fell. It was starting to get dark. The smell of freshly mowed grass drifted to them on a light breeze.

Vanessa was watching him, nodding slowly. "I'm not proud of it," she said, "but I was involved with him. There was more to it, but yeah."

"Wow."

Tears gathered in her eyes. "I was sad when he passed away. We weren't intimate anymore, but he remained a, well, kind of a friend."

Luke frowned. Why was his sister showing more emotion about the loss of old Oscar than Angie had?

"You hate me," she said, her mouth working.

"No." He squeezed her hand briefly. Vanessa's mistakes were a product of their upbringing. Somewhere along the line, her ideas about right and wrong, and her sense of her own value as a woman, had gotten lost. "It's not my place to judge. That's up to God. We've all made mistakes, but we're forgiven if we repent, thanks to Jesus."

"I hope so." She wiped her eyes and stood. "I'd better go in. Thanks for doing all this work on my house and for... for understanding."

He hugged her, said goodbye to Declan and gathered his things, still reeling from the shock of Vanessa's revelation.

It was even more reason why he shouldn't get too close with Angie.

Chapter Four

Friday morning was beautiful, a perfect May day. To Angie's surprise, and against her better judgment, she was in Luke's truck, riding shotgun with the window open.

Peppy rode in the back seat, her dog booster seat safely strapped in. Her nose was lifted, her ears blowing in the breeze.

Luke had one arm out the window. He drove in a relaxed way, as if he were comfortable in his own skin. Even when another driver passed him and pulled in too close, Luke braked gently and glanced back to make sure Peppy was secure. He didn't get all full of road rage like some men tended to do.

Like Oscar had tended to do.

"Thank you for coming along and for driving," she said. "I appreciate it."

"It worked out," he said easily. "I'd planned to be off today and tomorrow to finish the cleanup and move in, but I got ahead. This will give me a jump start on understanding your project."

"I need to pin down more details myself," she admitted. "I'll pay you, of course."

"No need," he said. "You're giving me free rent. I'm happy to help."

She shook her head. "I insist. This isn't about the carriage house. This is about the paid project."

"We'll talk about it," he said easily.

Yes, we will, and I'll pay you. She had to.

She wanted to make sure things stayed professional between them. On such a pretty day, dressed in casual jeans and with Peppy riding along, it would be all too easy to look at this as a fun excursion.

A fun excursion with a handsome man.

Peppy yipped from the back seat.

Luke glanced back. "Happy dog," he commented.

"She is," Angie said, reaching back to rub Peppy's head. "That's part of what makes her a great therapy dog. Her positive attitude rubs off on the people she visits."

Luke nodded. "My nephew was talking about having her visit his class. He loved it."

"Declan, right?"

Luke nodded.

"He seems like a sweet boy. He was disappointed that he didn't get to read to Peppy, but he didn't make a fuss about it."

"He's pretty happy that he'll be able to visit Peppy when I'm living in your carriage house," Luke said. He glanced over at her. "I mean, I don't want to assume. We—me and Declan—won't get in your way. It's just, if Peppy is out sometime, maybe Declan can—"

"Of course," Angie interrupted. "Peppy would love it if Declan played with her some, and I would, too. We only do therapy visits two or three times per week, and the rest of the time, she could use a little more play than I have time to give."

"That's great, then," he said. "Declan won't be around this weekend, I don't think. He's not old enough to be a help with moving, but he's old enough to get in the way. He'll be with his mom."

"You're close with your sister?"

A shadow crossed his face. "I am," he said.

"Maybe I'll meet her sometime," she said.

He paused. "Maybe," he said finally. "Hey, is that the training place up there?" He pointed to a sign.

"That's it." Angie's face heated. She'd been enjoying this ride so much that she'd forgotten to look for the place. But Luke had gone cool when she'd mentioned meeting his sister. He must want to keep things on a professional level rather than a personal one, too. And that was a good thing.

They pulled up to a large converted barn surrounded by fields that overlooked the bay.

A woman with short-cropped gray hair walked briskly toward them. "You're late," she said.

Angie blinked. "I'm sorry," she said and checked her phone. "I thought our appointment was at ten o'clock."

"It's 10:02," the woman said.

"My apologies," she said, and introduced Luke and Peppy. "I'm looking forward to seeing your training area."

"This way." She marched ahead of them, leading them inside. Green turf covered the floor, and a fence separated the training area from the reception area. In the training area was a ramp and a tunnel and a set of hurdles. "We do agility training here, too, but our main thing is puppy and dog obedience training." She snapped her fingers at Peppy. "Sit," she ordered.

Peppy glanced up at Angie and slowly sat.

"Down," the woman ordered.

Peppy lay down, again slowly.

The woman walked a few steps away and snapped her fingers again. "Come," she said.

Peppy stood and trotted behind Angie.

The woman repeated her command.

Peppy cowered.

"I, um, was hoping to look around the place a little," Angie said. "Peppy's solidly trained already."

"Is she?" The woman lifted her nose. She then led them around, showing the runs outside and the training equipment. When they came back inside, two dogs barked from their crates, but a finger snap from their trainer made them lie down, silent.

Angie felt sorry for them. She wasn't a strict trainer herself. Not even a real dog trainer, just a self-educated one with a love for dogs and dog therapy work. "It's a beautiful facility," she said. "Thank you for showing it to us."

"Of course." The woman frowned and studied Peppy then Angie. "If you need any of your therapy dogs more thoroughly trained, give me a call."

"I will. Thank you again."

They drove away, and once they were on the road again, Luke glanced over at Angie just as she looked at him. They both burst into laughter.

"I'm glad I'm not a dog," Luke said. "I'd be terrified to go there."

"Same," Angie said. "My training style is a lot different. I may hire a certified trainer at some point, but not one quite that strict."

"I'm glad. Next place on the list?"

"The rescue where I got Peppy," she said and punched the address into the GPS. Twenty minutes later, they were there.

Before Angie could climb out of the truck, Luke was opening her door for her. He held out a hand and helped her down, gentlemanly behavior that made her heart beat a little faster. She met his eyes and saw that he was looking at her with a certain male awareness.

She wished she wasn't quite so familiar with that expression on a man's face.

She dropped his hand and hurried to get Peppy out of the truck. She needed to stop paying attention to how nice and handsome Luke was.

Inside the animal shelter, Louwana Jones stood as soon as she saw them. She enfolded Angie in her arms, then picked up Peppy and held out a hand to Luke as Angie introduced them.

"It's great to see you," she said. "I know you're just here to look at our setup. But if you happen to see a pup who tugs at your heart, let me know. We have a lot of dogs right now. Cats upstairs, too, if you're interested."

She led them into the kennel area, and immediately, a deafening amount of barking overrode any attempts at conversation. Peppy nuzzled in Louwana's arms.

Angie walked along slowly, trying to focus on the layout but getting more caught up in the dogs. A couple of small white dogs, in a kennel together, barked and yipped and pawed at the front of their cages, and Angie knelt to pet and talk to them.

Luke was at the next kennel over, kneeling to coax a cowering pit bull toward him.

"Give him a treat," Louwana advised and handed Luke a couple of small dog biscuits from her pocket. Luke tossed one in, and the dog came forward, grabbed it and retreated to the back of the cage. He repeated that, a little closer, and the dog crawled forward to get it and retreated again.

"Do that about twenty more times, and he'll get a little friendlier," Louwana said.

"I'll be back to see you, buddy," Luke said as they moved on.

They talked to Louwana about the pros and cons of how the kennel was laid out, and she gave suggestions for keeping a smaller number of dogs.

By the time they'd finished looking at everything and talking with the chatty Louwana and a couple of volunteers, it was one o'clock and Angie was starving. "Any interest in a quick lunch before we head back?" she asked. "I have a therapy visit to do with Peppy this afternoon, but I need a bite to eat."

"Sure thing. Where do you have in mind?"

"There's a diner…" She told him where.

"And where are you visiting after that?"

"An assisted-living place."

"Can I come?"

Angie was shocked that he was interested. "I mean, if you want to," she said, studying him, trying to understand his motivations.

"I'd like to get a better idea of what therapy dogs do," he said. "Plus, it's a nice day, and I'm enjoying being with you."

Angie looked at him, startled, and their gazes held for a second too long. What on earth? He sounded like…wow. Like he was flirting. Maybe he'd thought her invitation to lunch opened that door?

If he were interested in her—the thought flattered and excited her—she had to shut it down. She couldn't be with a man like him. It would only lead to heartbreak when he learned about her past.

She straightened, lifted her chin. "You're welcome to come, and of course, I'll pay you for your time."

"We already talked about that," he said. "I'm doing this because I want to."

She couldn't help the bolt of excitement that shot through her. That a man like Luke would want to spend time understanding her world…it was intoxicating. She blew out a breath and grasped for a sense of professionalism. "Then lunch is on me, at least."

"That, I'll agree to," he said. "But be warned, I have a big appetite."

She lifted an eyebrow. "Why am I not surprised?"

All she meant was that he was a big guy, but when he smiled, she realized he might have thought she was flirting.

She looked away. No way was she letting that happen with a man like Luke Johnson. Morally, at least, he was way, way out of her league.

After reluctantly letting Angie pay the tab for their lunch, Luke drove them to the assisted-living center where her therapy-dog visit was to take place.

It was a large, red-brick complex. Planters sported blue and yellow flowers, and through the fence Luke glimpsed a courtyard with benches and a little pond. Several people lingered by the front desk, chatting. If he hadn't known the purpose of the place, he'd have thought it was like any other fancy apartment building on the Eastern Shore. The only visible difference was that everyone had white hair.

As he walked beside Angie and Peppy, Luke reminded himself why he was here. It wasn't to get to know Angie better, no way. It was to understand her work so that he could do a better job of building her kennel and dog runs.

Even the thought set off his internal malarkey detector. Visiting a senior center had nothing to do with building a dog kennel.

They were getting along well. Too well. They seemed to laugh at the same things and to share a similar level of energy. He found her very attractive; that was no surprise. But she also seemed to enjoy being with him.

If everything else were equal, if they'd been on similar financial levels and if there were no baggage between them, he'd have asked her out in a heartbeat.

But he couldn't do that. She was wealthy and he was struggling. Even worse, he knew a horrible secret about her late husband, whom she seemed to have adored.

The man had been a cheater. And not just with the kind of random women Luke had seen when he'd worked on Oscar's house; he'd cheated with Luke's sister.

That was a good reason to keep his distance from her. Not admire her red hair glinting in the May sunshine as she walked alongside him, chatting about various therapy visits she'd been on.

Inside the building, she proceeded to a lobby, checked them in and then beckoned him down the hall to a large lounge area where the visit was to take place.

"Angie!" Several people rushed over when they saw her, and Luke watched, interested. Ostensibly, Peppy was the hit. But Angie appeared to be just as much the reason people were happy about the visit. She had a smile for everyone, remembered names, asked after a couple of residents who weren't here.

The dog provided a vehicle for conversation for some of the quieter residents, and Angie seemed to seek them out. She lifted Peppy and placed her gently on the lap of a woman in a wheelchair, making sure there was a soft blanket on the woman's lap first so that the dog's claws didn't dig into tender skin. She discouraged one of the residents from picking Peppy up and carrying her around, explaining that the dog was a little shy and preferred to be carried by someone she knew.

The energy in the room was elevated just by having Angie and Peppy there, and Luke was newly determined to do a good job for her. This kind of work was obviously important. If Angie could train more dogs and handlers, more people could be helped by the presence of teams like Angie and Peppy.

"Who's the handsome guy?" one of the ladies asked in a loud voice. "Is that your new boyfriend?"

Angie laughed a little and looked over at Luke. "No, he's better than a boyfriend. He's a handyman, and he's going to be building a kennel at my house so I can have more dogs like Peppy."

"That's what we were talking about before, Steffy," another woman said. "Angie, we collected some money to help you get started with your new program." She reached into her enormous bag and pulled out an envelope bulging with small bills.

"That's so kind of you!" Angie seemed surprised and almost overcome. "I appreciate it so much."

The woman who'd commented about Luke leaned forward. "Our crochet group is having a sale. We could donate that money to your cause, too."

Angie hugged her. "You donate wherever your group wants to. I know you always support good causes."

As a couple of women enjoyed Peppy's company, a man in a wheelchair buzzed over to Angie. "How's Oscar, that old rascal?" he asked, bushy gray eyebrows working up and down.

"Oh, Pete. I didn't know you were living here now." Angie sat down on a chair and took the older man's hand. "I'm surprised you haven't heard. Oscar passed away more than a year ago."

The man huffed out a breath. "He was too young to go. Only seventy, wasn't he?"

"Not even," Angie said, swallowing hard. "He was way too young to go."

"Pancreatic cancer," another man said. "You knew that, Pete."

The man nodded. "I guess I did. Hard to keep everything straight. I'm sorry, young lady."

"It's okay." She pulled her hand away, and Luke noticed that it took a little effort. The man didn't want to let go. He scooted his wheelchair closer, effectively trapping her.

Luke was just here as an observer, but he could tell that Angie was starting to feel a little stressed.

He walked over to the ladies who were playing with Peppy. "Would you mind if we gave Peppy back to Angie for a minute?" he asked.

One of the women looked over and rolled her eyes. "If Pete has her cornered, she needs a therapy dog," she said and handed Peppy's leash to Luke.

As he walked over, Pete was leaning closer, saying something to Angie that made her lean away with an artificial smile. She looked around and seemed relieved to lay eyes on Luke and Peppy.

Luke brought the dog to her and handed her the leash.

Pete grabbed Luke's sleeve. "You knew her husband, Oscar?" he asked.

"No, I didn't," Luke said. It wasn't a lie. Although he'd done some work for Oscar, he'd barely spoken with the man aside from a few minutes of instruction about the project being completed in his home.

"He was a smart one to catch this pretty little fish," the old man said, nodding at Angie, "even if he caught her in a dirty pond."

What did *that* mean? Nothing good, that was for sure.

Angie stood. "It's about time for us to leave," she said. There was a high spot of color on each of her cheeks.

"He sure liked to run around, liked the ladies," Pete said. "Sad such a fun guy is gone so soon."

Angie backed away, spun and gave a general wave to the room. "Peppy and I have to go, but we'll be back next month," she said.

Amidst a flurry of thanks, they left.

As they walked out of the building, Luke could see from Angie's expression that she was upset.

"That guy seemed like a jerk," Luke said. "Was he really even a friend of your husband?"

Angie hesitated. "He was," she said finally. "But not a close friend, and obviously, he got a lot of things wrong. Oscar was a good guy."

Luke questioned that. Besides what he'd seen with his own eyes while working on their house years ago, he now knew that Angie's husband had been intimate with Vanessa while married to Angie. Apparently his friends, like this Pete character, knew Oscar had been a ladies' man.

It seemed like Angie believed the best of her late husband, and it certainly wasn't Luke's place to make her question that.

In fact, the opposite. If other people knew things about Oscar that Angie didn't, Luke felt a strong urge to protect her from those unpleasant truths.

Don't be a hero. She wasn't for him, and her state of mind, her happiness, weren't his responsibility nor his concern.

He just had to figure out how to remember that when all he wanted to do was pull her into his arms, protect her from pain and offer comfort.

Staying away wasn't going to be easy, considering that he was moving onto her property tomorrow.

Chapter Five

Saturday morning, Angie had just taken her coffee and newspaper out onto the deck when she heard Luke's truck pull up to the carriage house. Peppy gave a couple of yips then flopped beside Angie.

Angie reached down to give Peppy's ears a quick rub. "You're not exactly a guard dog, are you?"

Peppy looked up at her and nudged her hand for more petting.

Angie had been trying not to think about yesterday, that visit to the assisted-living place that had started out so well. And then had come Pete's awful words: *He found her in a dirty pond.*

What he'd said, combined with his leering, had made her feel unclean. To top it off, Luke had heard the remark. Which shouldn't matter, but it did.

The sound of the truck door slamming got Peppy's attention, and she went to the edge of the deck and gave another yip. Angie stepped into her ancient yard sandals, and they both walked over to greet Luke.

Luke let down the tailgate of his truck. Boxes and furniture lined the truck bed.

"Can I help?" Angie asked.

"Definitely not." He flashed her a smile that made her

suck in her breath. The man had a seriously great smile. "I can get this stuff," he continued. "You sit back and relax. Be a lady of leisure."

She snorted, picked up Peppy and retreated to the back deck. Not before she noticed that Luke was wearing his cross necklace. Again.

Luke seemed at least mildly attracted to her. She knew men well enough to figure that out. She was attracted, too.

Which made this pure foolishness, having him live here. There was no way they could be together. Luke wasn't a worldly, sophisticated guy like Oscar had been. He wouldn't understand her past.

"Hey there!" Brian and Elizabeth, her next-door neighbors, waved from their side of the fence. Brian was a retired accountant, and Elizabeth a nurse who worked part-time. They were lovely, both in their sixties, and they'd been super welcoming when she'd moved in last year.

She waved back, and the pair took that as invitation to come over.

"Need a hand?" Brian asked Luke.

"That would be great." Luke was up in his truck shifting a dresser toward the back. Brian grabbed one end, and the two men carried the piece into the carriage house.

"Huh. He wouldn't let *me* help," Angie said to Elizabeth.

"And rightly so." The older woman joined Angie on the deck, opening a Tupperware container to reveal a dozen slices of coffee cake. "Have some," she said. "Brian and I can't eat all of this."

"Yum. Thank you." Angie took a bite and closed her eyes as the cinnamon-and-butter filling almost exploded in her mouth. "Wow. This is great. Want some coffee?"

"Sure thing."

Angie made a full pot and brought it out. Brian and Luke

had come over and were scarfing down coffee cake. She poured them both coffee, and after drinking it, they went back to work.

"How's the therapy-dog program coming along?" Elizabeth asked. Angie had talked to Brian and Elizabeth about it before deciding to move forward, since they were her closest neighbors and would be affected by having more dogs next door.

"I have more work to do with fundraising, but as soon as we get the kennel built—maybe even before that—I'm going to add a couple more dogs. I want to recruit a couple of handlers and get their training started."

"You know," Elizabeth said, "Brian would be a good part of a therapy team. He likes dogs, and he needs more to do since he retired."

"That would be wonderful!" There were almost always more women than men who wanted to do dog therapy work, but men fit in better at certain locations.

"Ask him, but don't tell him I suggested it. He gets irritated when I try to find him things to do, but he needs it."

"I noticed he mows the lawn every few days," Angie said, laughing.

"Right?" Elizabeth laughed, too. "It's ridiculous. But I can't criticize him. He's always been a hard worker. It just got to be too much, working the tax season year after year. I'm so glad he retired."

As they sipped coffee and watched the men carry boxes into the carriage house, Angie couldn't help envying Elizabeth's relationship with Brian. It was built on a solid foundation. They went dancing, and she'd seen them kissing on their back porch, but there was more to it than romance. They were best friends.

With all her heart, Angie wanted that for herself. Wanted someone to care for her because of who she was, not just because of how she looked. Oscar had come to care for her that way—sort of—but she knew very well that her looks and youth had been the most important things she'd brought to the marriage.

Without being too obvious about it, she watched Luke. His jeans and work boots were no fuss, but fuss wasn't needed for him to look amazing. His muscular arms stretched the sleeves of his T-shirt, and he moved with a natural grace. Angie had had a good time with him yesterday before everything had gone south at the assisted-living place. He'd hung out with her and paid attention and laughed easily.

Now, he seemed to be having fun with Brian. The two men talked and laughed as they carried things into the carriage house.

"Any romantic possibilities between you and Luke?" Elizabeth asked.

Angie looked away from Luke, heat rising to her cheeks as she met Elizabeth's eyes. "No. He's a great guy, or he seems to be. I don't know him all that well. But it's strictly business between us."

"Everyone needs love," Elizabeth said gently.

"But not everyone gets it," Angie replied. "Some of us have to be content with less."

Elizabeth gave her a sympathetic smile and leaned down to pet Peppy, and Angie was thankful the woman respected her enough not to push.

Half an hour later, Luke and Brian strolled over. "We're done," Brian said. "Any coffee cake left?" He patted his ample belly. "I worked up an appetite."

"Me, too," Luke said.

Elizabeth handed over the container, and the two men grabbed the remaining slices while Angie refilled their coffee mugs.

"We're headed out to do some errands in a bit," Elizabeth said, "but would the two of you like to come over tonight? Nothing fancy, but we're grilling burgers and veggies."

Angie froze. She'd known she would see more of Luke when he moved in, but she'd figured it would be on a professional basis. Going to a neighbor's cookout was social.

"I'm up for it," Luke said immediately. "I'm not a good cook, and since I knew I was moving, I didn't stock up on my usual assortment of frozen food and cans of soup."

"This will be better than that," Elizabeth said. "We'll convert you to better food here on Hanover Street."

"Lots of cookouts and block parties," Brian said.

"Sounds good to me, while I'm here," Luke said.

"Angie? You in?" Elizabeth's eyes were dancing.

Angie tilted her head to one side, studying her friend. She suspected the woman was matchmaking, and she didn't appreciate it. But she also didn't want to be rude, especially since Elizabeth had brought over that wonderful coffee cake and Brian had helped Luke move. "Uh, okay, sure," she said weakly.

It looked like Luke was game to become part of the neighborhood's social life. Now they were going to dinner together.

How was she supposed to keep a distance?

As he shaved and dressed for the neighbors' cookout that night, Luke regretted his earlier enthusiasm for it. Why had he acted like he fit in with these classy people?

He didn't want to go.

He'd spent half the afternoon working on the carriage house, getting some stuck windows operative and doing a couple of simple wiring fixes. Then he'd talked to Angie—on the phone, not in person—about what she wanted in the kennel and dog runs, and priced some wood and other supplies online.

Now, he was tired. He'd just as soon settle into his new home with a good book or a TV documentary.

But Angie was expecting him to go, and the neighbors were, and they did seem like nice folks. So once he was ready, he went downstairs and then walked across the lawn to Angie's place. He felt awkward, like he was a high-school kid going to pick up a girl for a date.

Not that he'd dated in high school, not really. He'd gotten together with some girls, but not for traditional, dinner-and-movie dates. More like meeting in the park with a six-pack. Those days were gone—he'd quit drinking about the same time he'd started going to church—but still, he'd never gotten the hang of dating the way that Angie had probably been used to.

She must have seen him coming because she emerged from her house before he could climb the steps to the front door. She was wearing a dress made colorful with all kinds of flowers, pink and red and blue. Her red hair flowed loose around her bare arms. She wore just enough makeup to make her green eyes even more striking than usual.

Luke's mouth went dry. She was a total knockout. What right did he have to spend an evening with someone like that?

And how could her jerk of a husband have ever wanted to stray from such an incredible woman?

"I hope you're hungry." She was carrying a plastic bowl, and she held it up. "I made a lot of potato salad."

"I love it." Her relaxed manner put him at ease. "I like anything I don't have to cook, but I especially love potatoes in all forms."

"Good." She swung into place beside him, and as they

walked together, he again had that date-like feeling. This time, he found himself enjoying it, at least a little.

Rather than knocking on the front door, Angie led him around to the back of the faux log cabin where Brian and Elizabeth were already out on the patio. Brian was lighting the grill, or trying to, and Elizabeth sat relaxing in an Adirondack chair, a glass of lemonade in her hand. She stood and welcomed them both with hugs. "Come have a seat," she said, gesturing toward the table, where a vegetable tray and chips and dip added a homey touch.

Luke thanked her but joined Brian at the grill. He was always more comfortable if there was something to do, and it looked like Brian was having trouble with the propane tank. Luke knelt to help him while the women talked in the background.

Brian and Elizabeth had a nice big yard, almost as big as Angie's, and Luke noticed a tire swing and a tetherball pole and a narrow creek with an arched wooden bridge over it. "Did you raise your kids here?" he asked.

"No. We married late, but Elizabeth has kids from a previous marriage, and now we host our grandsons as often as we can."

"Sweet," Luke said.

"Those boys are adorable," Angie chimed in from the table. "In fact," she said, turning to Elizabeth, "isn't your middle grandson in second grade?"

"He is," Elizabeth said.

"Luke's nephew may spend some time over here, and he's the same age. Maybe the boys could play together."

"Wonderful," Elizabeth said.

"The more, the merrier," Brian added. "We love kids."

"It's a great place for them." Luke suppressed a sigh. He

wished Declan didn't have to play in the street. The kid would love to be able to run around a backyard like this.

Vanessa would like it here, too. Maybe he'd have Vanessa and Declan both over soon, only if Vanessa met Angie…talk about awkward. Angie wouldn't know about Vanessa's role in her husband's life, but Vanessa would know that Angie was the woman who'd been married to the man she'd been seeing. Would that set her back emotionally? Would she blurt out some memory of old Oscar, clueing Angie in on the too-close relationship she'd had with the man?

"Don't you think so, Luke?" Elizabeth was asking.

He shook his head to clear it. "Sorry, I missed what you were saying. Space case."

"You've had a long day," Elizabeth said, smiling at him. "I was suggesting that Angie and Peppy participate in the Memorial Day parade to raise awareness of therapy dogs and her program."

Angie shook her head. "I don't think so."

Elizabeth started setting the table, putting out silverware and colorful cloth napkins. "Why not?"

"It's not just a general parade," Angie said. "It's about those who lost their lives fighting for our country. I'll go to the parade and the ceremony, but it wouldn't be right for me to participate."

"Bravo," Luke said. "Most people think Memorial Day is about the start of summer, but it's more than that."

"Vet?" Brian asked. He put hamburger patties on the grill then sprinkled them with seasoning.

Luke nodded. "Afghanistan. You?"

Brian nodded. "Spent some time in Lebanon."

Elizabeth grimaced. "Rough time in your life, Luke, I imagine. I know it was in Brian's."

"Well… I got to see more of the world than I otherwise

would have." Luke smiled, making light of it. "But yeah, it was bad over there at times. I came home without major injuries or PTSD, but other guys weren't as fortunate."

They were quiet as they sat down and started their meal. Luke was thinking about a couple of friends he'd lost. His own father, too, though not in quite the same way.

Brian must have been thinking along similar lines. "You ever visit veterans' groups or hospitals with Peppy?" he asked Angie.

"I'd like to," she said, "but Peppy and I have our hands full with kids' reading programs. Peppy does so well with kids." She paused, then added, "But when I get more dogs, *you* could be part of a therapy-dog team and go to the VA. You'd be great at it."

Luke saw Elizabeth give Angie a subtle thumbs-up. Interesting.

"Hmm, I might think about that," Brian said.

The conversation moved on, light and easy. Everyone helped clean up, and then Brian lit the gas fire pit. With the cushioned benches around it, a couple of ottomans to prop your feet, folded blankets in case the night air got cold… yeah. This was a nice setup. Even nicer was the way Brian and Elizabeth sat close together, cuddled up on a love seat. It wasn't all that common, in Luke's world at least, to see an older married couple that liked each other enough to be so openly affectionate.

As the sky darkened and birds chirped and chattered their sunset songs, Luke watched Angie. She was so pretty as she leaned toward the fire, warming up, talking with animation.

He wanted to put an arm around her, to draw her close like Brian and Elizabeth. It took more effort than it should have to resist. But the talk was casual and pleasant, and the air was warm, and Luke felt, if not fulfilled, then peaceful.

They walked back to Angie's property together, through the gate that separated Elizabeth and Brian's place from hers. It was a little chilly, so he took off the flannel he'd worn over his T-shirt and draped it over Angie's shoulders.

"But you'll be cold," she said, already snuggling into the garment.

"I'm fine," he said. "Warm-blooded."

"Surprise, surprise," she said with a smile. It was one of those occasional comments she made that could be interpreted as flirting and bespoke more knowledge of the world than he'd have expected from a rich, sheltered wife.

He wanted to put an arm around her. Wanted to kiss her. But he couldn't. He knew too much that she didn't know, and to get involved with her in the face of the secret facts he knew about her husband would lead to all kinds of bad possible outcomes. He cast around for a neutral topic of conversation. Realizing tomorrow was Sunday, he asked her what church she attended.

Her steps slowed. "I don't," she said.

"Oh! I thought…" He trailed off. Why had he thought she was a believer?

"I read the Bible every day," she said. "I pray. And I sometimes watch a church service on TV. But I just don't… I'm not the organized religion type, I guess."

That didn't ring true to him. "Want to go to church with me?" he was shocked to hear himself ask.

Angie stared at Luke, trying to make out whether he was serious or not about inviting her to church.

Clouds drifted over the moon, casting his handsome face into shadow. Peppy strained on the leash, drawn to some nighttime creature rustling through the bushes, so Angie picked the dog up in her arms, giving herself a moment to think.

Did she want to go to church with Luke?

The thought of it aroused so many mixed emotions that she could barely untangle them. Pleasure, that he'd asked her to spend time with him. Worry, that like others in her past, he was looking at her as a project, a heathen who needed saving. Discomfort at the very thought of walking into a church.

Aside from a few weddings and funerals, she'd spent almost no time inside a church. Never attended a regular Sunday service.

They walked slowly forward, past the carriage house. Luke beckoned her over, sat down on the steps of it and patted the step beside him. "It's not a complicated question," he said. "Don't overthink it."

"It's a very kind invitation," she said. "But I don't think so."

"Why?" he probed. He was looking at her with those intense brown eyes. "If you're a person of faith, don't you want to have a faith community?"

The thought of that sounded wonderful, actually; it was just that she didn't believe it could happen, not for her. She smiled, trying to lighten up the sudden heaviness of the discussion. "It's complicated, like the kids say."

"Complicated how?"

He wasn't going to let up on her, obviously. "I had a few bad experiences with church," she said. Then she waited for him to discount her claim.

Instead, he shook his head. "That stinks," he said. "Sometimes Christians are the worst advertisement for Christianity."

The unexpectedness of his response made her smile. "That's for sure," she said. She thought of the high-minded women that had come to visit the club where she'd danced. How they'd passed out tracts about sin and salvation and told the girls they needed to get to church, right away, lest they burn for eternity.

It hadn't been a good sales pitch, but she and another girl had still been intrigued enough to attend one Sunday. They hadn't even gone home from work, since their work ran so late. They'd just changed clothes and showed up at the earliest service.

A few people had greeted them, but others had stared. Angie had looked down at her T-shirt and jeans, wondering if she had inadvertently worn something see-through.

She hadn't, but the other people were more dressed up. "This is giving me the creeps," her friend had said. As soon as everyone had stood for an opening hymn, they'd sneaked out.

"Want to talk about it?" Luke asked.

"About what?"

"About your bad experiences in church. I kinda lost you there, got the feeling you were delving into the past."

"I was," she admitted. "I just…remember feeling uncomfortable, stared at."

"You're very pretty," Luke said. "Maybe that's why they were staring."

Angie's face heated. She was glad Luke thought she was pretty, but it wasn't what she wanted to be known for, given her past. "I did have a pastor hit on me once," she said. Trying to make a joke, but it wasn't funny enough.

Luke shook his head and put a hand over hers. "I'm sorry that happened."

She was touched that he actually believed her. "Men are men," she said. When his eyes opened wider and he raised an eyebrow, she clapped a hand over her mouth. "I didn't mean all men are alike, didn't mean to accuse you of anything. It's just, pastors are people, and some of them act, you know, the way men act." She felt her face heat again and shook her head, laughing a little. "I'm digging myself in deeper, here, aren't I?"

"Yeah." He was studying her with curiosity. "But as far as church, didn't your husband belong to a church?"

"He did," she said. "But he knew I was uncomfortable with it, and he was fine with not going."

"Hmmm." An expression of disapproval flashed across Luke's face and then was gone.

"He prayed," she said, feeling defensive of Oscar. "When he was so sick, we prayed together sometimes, and a nice pastor came and visited him in the hospital. I think he was right with God."

"What about you?" Luke asked. "Is that how you want to live your life, going forward? Having a bad impression of church and not having the comfort of a faith community?"

"Well, when you put it that way…" She was trying to make another joke, but once again, it fell flat. "Actually, I'd like to have a faith community, but the couple of times I've tried have scared me off."

"Let my church change your mind."

"Why are you so into me coming to church with you?"

He looked at her for a long moment. "Maybe it seems like I'm trying to hit on you, just like that pastor did," he said. "And it's true that you're a beautiful, intriguing woman. If things were different, I might be doing that. But they're not. And in any case, I would never use church to lure you into doing something you didn't want to do."

She studied his face, her heart pounding to the rhythm of the words echoing in her head. *You're a beautiful, intriguing woman. If things were different…*

What things? she wondered. What would need to be different for Luke to actually ask her out? Could he somehow see her soiled past?

"My church is really friendly," he said, "and not just to people who dress up and know all the words to the songs. Local fishermen come in right off the water sometimes. Teenagers wear their ripped jeans. The music team is terrific, and the pastor isn't boring like the ones I remember from childhood." He paused, then added, "And I can promise he won't hit on you. He's very happily married."

"It sounds nice," she said, meaning it.

"I don't want to push too hard," he said, "but the invitation is there. I'll be leaving about nine fifteen, and if you want, I'll knock on your door on the way out, see if you've changed your mind."

He was sweet, and persuasive. And the picture he'd painted of his church aroused a surprising longing in her.

"I don't know what to wear," she said, staring at her knees. "You mentioned what the fishermen wear and the teenagers, but it's women who tend to get judgy about clothes."

He chuckled, a rich, warm sound.

"Are you laughing at me?" she asked.

"No. I'm thinking about how I felt the same way, getting ready for a cookout with your wealthy friends. I didn't know what to wear."

She took the opportunity to look him up and down. "You look just right," she said. "And anyway, it didn't matter what you wore to Brian and Elizabeth's. They wouldn't judge. They're not that kind of people."

"My church mates wouldn't judge you, either," he said.

They looked at each other, and Angie found she couldn't pull her eyes away. A spark seemed to travel from his warm eyes to her fast-beating heart.

If things were different, he might have kissed her, she thought.

But that wasn't happening. So she had to make a decision about church independent of any of those types of feelings.

Maybe he pitied her. Maybe he sensed that she was a bad woman with a bad past. Maybe he thought, like others did, that she'd only married Oscar for his money and that she was a money-grubbing type, a gold digger in need of forgiveness.

Trying to figure out his motives—anyone's motives—was a losing battle. The proposition on the table in front of her was about something else: faith.

And she did long to be closer to the Lord, to know Him better. There was only so far she could go on her own. "All right," she heard herself saying. "I'll be ready at nine fifteen."

Chapter Six

"That wasn't so bad, was it?"

Angie smiled up at Luke. "It was a beautiful service." She wasn't exaggerating.

Bayside Chapel was a small, white, weathered building on a flat spit of land that jutted out into the Chesapeake Bay. Aside from a couple of accents, the windows were clear glass, giving unobstructed views of the surrounding water. The service had included lots of enthusiastic singing, accompanied by a piano and guitar rather than the solemn-sounding organs she remembered from weddings and funerals she'd attended. A short sermon on the Epistle of James made her think. Hearing the Bible passages read out loud made for a completely different kind of experience than she had sitting propped up in bed with her daily devotion and scripture readings.

The service had added a new dimension to her faith, and she thought she might like to come back. Especially since people had been warm and welcoming but hadn't seemed to single her out or focus on her.

Everyone was headed toward the covered pavilion beside the church, where tables were laden with a variety of covered dishes. A soft breeze ruffled the edges of red-checkered tablecloths. Kids ran on the lawn beside the pavilion, some

playing tag, some tossing a ball. "Want to have lunch here?"
Luke asked. "Beats cooking."

She laughed. "I'm detecting a theme with you," she said.
"The less cooking, the better." Then, noticing that all the
food was homemade, she frowned. "But we didn't bring
anything."

"That's okay," he said. "I usually just make a donation."
After leading the way to a wooden box with a slit in the top,
he reached for his wallet.

"Let me." Angie fumbled with her purse.

Luke put a hand on her arm. "I've got this. You're my
guest."

"But—"

"Angie." His voice went cool. "I can afford the donation
for your lunch."

She looked over to see that his jawline was rigid. She'd
offended him. "I didn't mean you couldn't afford it, I just
wanted…never mind. Thank you."

Obviously, Luke was sensitive about money. He seemed
to be short of it, even though he worked hard, and she suspected that had to do with the financial contributions he
made to his sister and nephew.

While Angie had had a few cash-flow issues, given the
problems with Oscar's will, she had a fine cushion and
enough investments that she didn't need to worry about her
future, not too much, anyway. She had time to get her feet
on the ground, to start her nonprofit and forgo a salary until
it was scaled up to where they could afford it.

As he turned away from the box, still looking annoyed,
she touched his arm. "I'm sorry. I do know what it is to be
looked at as poor. I'm not there now, thanks to Oscar, but
it's not as if I did anything to earn what little bit of wealth
I have."

He gave her a strange look. "You may not have earned it, but you paid for it."

What was that supposed to mean?

He smiled at her, relaxed again. "Come on. Bayside Chapel has some seriously good cooks in the congregation."

He wasn't wrong. In addition to standard picnic offerings of pasta salad and hot dogs, there were crab cakes and crispy hush puppies and rockfish bites. On the dessert table were slices of sweet potato pie and multilayered Smith Island cake, yellow with chocolate icing. A big tray of homemade chocolate chip cookies was already being decimated by hungry kids.

Luke and Angie took their laden plates to the end of a long picnic table, and people immediately shifted over so they could sit down. Across from Luke, Angie alternated between savoring the food, enjoying the view of the sparkling bay and watching Luke interact with others.

He was ridiculously good-looking. Today he wore a dress shirt with sleeves rolled up, dark dress pants and leather shoes. He looked a little more formal than some of the churchgoers, and it suited him. As did his ready smile.

She could tell he was popular from the number of people who stopped by to greet him. A couple of men thanked him for work he'd done at the church, and an older lady who used a walker pinched his cheek and told him he was a "good young man" for cleaning out her gutters. So he helped out here at the church and in the community, in addition to helping his sister with her son.

Luke might not be all that young, but he was a good man, like the older woman had said. A good guy. As he talked and laughed easily with other members of the congregation, Angie felt almost proud to be the guest he'd brought to the church potluck.

"Angie?" Someone tapped on her shoulder.

She turned and squinted at the woman behind her. The same age as her and with a familiar face Angie couldn't place.

"I thought that was you! I'm Karen Wycliffe, remember? From the old neighborhood?"

Angie blinked as the years fell away. "Oh, Karen!" She stood and hugged the woman, and they walked to a less-crowded part of the pavilion. "What are you doing here?"

"I moved here a few years ago." Karen fluffed her hair off the back of her neck, a trademark gesture exactly the same as she'd done at eight years old. "How funny that we ended up in the same place. Do you like it? How long have you lived here? Are you working locally?"

Angie smiled at the multiple questions, something else Karen had done since she was a little girl. "I love it here. I moved here with my husband a few years ago."

Karen glanced over at Luke, who was talking to a couple of men, and her eyebrows lifted. "Wow. He's good-looking."

Angie laughed, her cheeks heating for some reason. "Oh! That's not my husband. My husband passed away."

"Oh, wow, I'm sorry!" The corners of Karen's mouth turned downward. "You haven't had an easy time of it."

Angie lifted her face to the cool breeze and smiled. "I'm doing okay. Really well, actually."

"Are you really? I've always worried about you. I mean, your stepfather was so…"

A brief image of the man, face twisted in a scowl, fist raised, flashed across Angie's mind. With the ease of long practice, she pushed it away. "I'm fine," she said. "That's all behind me. It was good for me to get out."

Karen shook her head, her eyes dark with sympathy. "I missed you so much, but I understood why you left."

A little girl ran up and pulled at Karen's hand. Karen hugged Angie again and then let the child tug her away, calling over her shoulder with a promise to stay in touch.

When Angie turned back toward the crowd, she realized Luke had come up beside her. He put a hand on her shoulder, the heat of it warming her. "Sorry I didn't get to talk with your friend," he said, "but I heard part of what she said. Something about your stepfather?"

"Yeah. He's the reason I left home young." She trailed off. This wasn't something she talked about, and she wasn't sure how to phrase it on a sunny Sunday afternoon at a church picnic.

Luke raised an eyebrow. "I'm listening, if you want to talk about it."

Did she? Normally, she kept her past to herself. But seeing Karen had brought back memories. And their corner of the picnic shelter had emptied out, giving them privacy. "He was a rough guy. In fact, he was indicted—this was after I got out—on charges that included attempted murder. The murder charge didn't stick, but he did some jail time, from what I heard."

"Wow." Distress crossed his face.

"Yeah. Not a fun person."

"You said you got out of the house? How young?"

She looked out at the sparkling bay, watched a sailboat dance along the horizon. "You know what? It's a beautiful day, and you just brought me to a wonderful church service. Let's just stay in the present."

"Of course," he said. "Sounds good to me. Come on, I'll introduce you to some folks."

So they chatted with people and ate too much dessert and enjoyed the sunshine. Someone brought out cornhole boards, and they both played, with Angie giving Luke a decent bit of competition.

As they left, one of the parishioners grabbed a hand of each of them. "I'm so glad you two came. We're very happy for you. You're such a nice couple."

"Oh, we're just friends," Angie said, feeling herself blush.

"We're not involved," he said quickly.

He'd said it so emphatically, too. Was there a reason?

From the church service, as well as from all her Bible reading, she knew she was forgiven in Christ. But if Luke knew her whole past, would that be forgivable?

Doubtful. Very doubtful.

She would enjoy the lovely friendship with an attractive man, and she wouldn't think about more.

On Sunday afternoon, Luke felt like lying down and listening to the baseball game on TV. But he couldn't. Today, since he had no jobs on his normal handyman rotation, he needed to make progress on Angie's fence.

You're doing this to help Vanessa, he reminded himself. *Vanessa and Declan. They're what matters.*

He used his auger to start the holes for the fence posts and then finished them off with the post hole digger.

The air was warm, and with his exertion, Luke was soon sweating. He'd take off his shirt, except that he didn't want to embarrass Angie. He had to be a pro here. He wasn't working as a friend.

He'd tried to be a friend by inviting Angie to church, and she'd seemed to enjoy it after an initial bit of anxiety at the church entryway. She'd mingled at the after-church picnic and spoken with the pastor. The adult Sunday school teacher had invited her to join her class, and she'd said she would think about it.

So he'd done his good deed, and what did he have to show for it? He'd made it so he might get to see Angie in his Sunday school class each and every week. No doubt wearing a cute sundress and sandals, with her pink toenails showing. Great.

Not that a man didn't like a nice view. Looking at pretty women was a fun pastime for a lot of men, Luke included, but Angie was more. There were depths to her, hidden emotions, a history she didn't always seem to want to talk about. She was almost…mysterious, and it was hooking him like a big fat worm would hook a trout.

"Hey, you're working too hard!"

Her smoky voice made him turn, and then he swallowed hard. She'd changed out of her church clothes into shorts and a red T-shirt and sneakers, and she was carrying a thermos and a plate. Peppy trotted along beside her.

"I brought you a snack and some lemonade. And an offer of help."

"Thank you." He felt tongue-tied in her presence. And he had to admit to himself that it wasn't the dress and sandals and painted toenails that had attracted him during church. None of that was in evidence now, but he still felt drawn to her. In fact, he could relate to Peppy, who was sitting at her feet, panting up at her.

He held a plastic glass while she poured, then drank the best lemonade he'd ever had. When he noticed a seed at the bottom of his glass, he realized why it was so good. "This is homemade?"

She nodded. "I love making lemonade from scratch. Cookies, too." She held out the plate.

"Chocolate chip? My favorite." He took a soft cookie and bit into chocolaty goodness.

Wow, it was great to be around someone who could bake.

She ate a cookie, too, while he told her about his progress. Peppy chased butterflies, leaping and snapping her jaws, wagging her tail.

"You're working so hard," she said once he'd explained what he was doing. "I can at least measure and carry and hold things. Won't an extra pair of hands make it easier? Plus, I'm strong." She held up an arm and flexed her bicep.

She was fit, no doubt, and she was also seriously cute. "Sure, it'll help," he admitted. But that wasn't the real reason he said yes. He wanted to be with her.

So they worked together. Luke did most of the drilling and digging, but she measured the holes he'd dug, making sure they were all the same depth. She helped him carry poles and stand them up. By the time they finished the section he'd intended to get done today, they were both sweating.

But with her working alongside him, it was fun. She didn't seem to mind the heat or the hard effort. Their eyes met often, and sometimes, their hands brushed together. They laughed at the antics of a pair of squirrels and Peppy's half-hearted pursuit of them.

The way she was acting…he didn't want to be one of those guys who thought every glance from a woman meant she wanted to marry him. But he was sensing that she enjoyed being with him. Maybe even was attracted to him.

When they lifted the last heavy fence post together and stuck it in the ground, their faces were close, and they didn't move apart. He couldn't, no matter that he knew he couldn't be involved.

Her lips were just inches from his, full and pretty. Her eyes were wide. She looked down and laughed a little, obviously aware.

His phone buzzed.

He took a step back. "I should get that in case…"

"Of course." She stepped back, too. Their eyes were locked together.

He looked at the lock screen. "It's my nephew." He took the call.

"Mom fell and she won't wake up," Declan said breathlessly.

"I'll be right there, buddy." Luke spun and strode toward his truck with the phone to his ear, fear flooding his chest. "Is she breathing? Remember how we held up a mirror?"

"I'll get one!"

Angie came up beside him, half-jogging to keep up with his pace. "Should I call 911?"

"Not yet." He got into the truck and put his phone on speaker. "You there, buddy?"

"Wait," Angie said, her voice breathless. "If you can wait one minute, I'll come with you. Maybe I can help." She plunked Peppy, the container of cookies and the thermos of lemonade into the back seat then ran inside. Seconds later, she was back with her purse.

Declan had returned to the phone. "I'm holding up the mirror. It's foggy."

"Good. She's breathing. I'll be there in ten minutes. Go get Mrs. Washington to come over."

"I want to stay with Mom." Declan's voice was subdued.

"Okay. Stay on the phone."

"I can't. It's about to die."

"Get off the phone and find a charger if you can. Call 911 if she seems worse. I'll be right there." He waited at a red light, tapping his fingers on the wheel, and peeled out as soon as it turned green.

"Do you know what's wrong?" Angie asked.

"She doesn't eat."

"You think it's low blood sugar?" She clung to the door as he accelerated around a turn.

"Anorexia. She's struggled with it in the past. Seems to be coming back."

"Oh…" Angie's voice sounded upset and soothing all at the same time. "I'm so sorry. That's serious, isn't it?"

"It can be." They'd reached Vanessa's neighborhood now, and Luke had to slow down. Lots of kids playing in the street, adults standing around talking, cars. He wove through, tooting his horn a couple of times. He wasn't trying to be a jerk, but he had to keep moving.

He pulled into the driveway of Vanessa's place and was out of the door and up the steps in seconds. He flung open the front door.

"Uncle Luke!" Declan rushed to him and grabbed his hand. "In the kitchen. She says her head hurts."

"She's awake?" They ran together through the house. He heard Angie behind him, heard the clicking of Peppy's claws on the wood floor.

In the kitchen, Vanessa had lifted herself up onto her elbows. "Luke," she whispered. "I fell."

He knelt beside her. "What hurts?"

"My tailbone. My head."

At least she was answering logically. He put an arm around Declan. "You did a good job, buddy."

"Is she gonna be okay?"

"Yeah." Luke prayed it was so. This time, yes, probably. He helped her to sit up, and she leaned against the cupboards. She reached out for Declan and stroked his hair, and he wrapped his arms around her and hugged her tightly. "You scared me, Mom!"

"I'm sorry." Her voice was a quarter of its usual volume. "I love you, baby."

It was a mark of how upset Declan was that he allowed himself to be called that without a fuss. Mother and son leaned back, their arms wrapped around each other.

Luke had forgotten about Peppy until the little dog walked boldly onto their laps and nudged his head against Declan's hand.

"Peppy!" Declan's voice sounded lighter, almost happy. "Mom, look, it's the reading dog I told you about!"

While the two of them petted and fussed over the dog, Luke stood, feeling exhausted. Angie was hanging back in the doorway. "You can come in," he said.

"Do you think a little lemonade would help her?" she asked.

"Maybe?" Vanessa had so many issues with food, but she needed to get something down. He didn't want her to try to walk without a little food in her body. He found a juice glass and held it for Angie to fill from her thermos. "Drink this," he said, handing it to Vanessa.

She sipped it. "Wow, this is good," she said and downed the glass. Then she frowned. "Was that full-sugar lemonade?"

"Yes, it was. I have cookies, too." Angie set down the Tupperware container on the table.

"Can I have some?" Declan was on his feet in an instant.

"Of course, honey, if it's okay with your mom."

"Can I have cookies, Mom?" Declan asked.

"Yeah, okay." Vanessa was looking a little more in control of herself now. She started to get up, and Luke quickly got next to her and held her elbow, steadying her and helping her into a chair at the table.

Declan was already on his second cookie.

"Would anyone like an actual meal, rather than just cookies?" Angie asked. "I'd be glad to cook."

Vanessa studied her. "I'm confused…who are you?"

"Sorry. I'm Angie Anderson."

Vanessa's eyes widened.

Sweat broke out across Luke's forehead. Was she going to reveal her past mistakes in front of Angie and Declan?

"Miss Angie brings Peppy to help us read," Declan said through a mouthful of cookie.

"And she's hired me to work on her carriage house and dog kennel," Luke said, trying to fill the empty air so Vanessa didn't have the space to blurt something out. "In fact, we were both working when Declan called. That's why we're sweaty."

"Maybe you could come over and visit Luke sometime," Angie said. "We have a nice outdoor fire pit, and you're welcome to use it." She looked from Luke to Vanessa and back again, including them both in the invitation.

"Let's make a fire and roast marshmallows!" Declan shouted.

"Inside voice," Luke said. But he was mostly grateful that Declan was recovering from his scare so well. It didn't hurt that Peppy had parked herself beside Declan's chair.

Vanessa was studying Angie. "You're such a nice woman, and pretty, too," she said. "I can't believe…"

Here it came. Luke tightened his stomach, bracing himself.

Peppy barked, and Declan broke off a piece of cookie. He held it out, and Angie cried, "No!" She grabbed Declan's hand. "She can't have chocolate, honey. It's bad for dogs."

Declan lowered his eyes. "I'm sorry. I didn't mean to hurt her."

"Don't worry, you didn't." Angie fumbled in her pocket. "Here. You can give her a couple of these treats. Make her work for them, though. She can sit and give paw and carry things."

As Declan played with Peppy, Luke focused on Vanessa. "I'd like for you to see a doctor," he said.

"No need." Vanessa waved a hand. "I'm fine. I just… forgot to eat."

Luke studied her narrowly.

"Hey, if you two need to talk," Angie said, "maybe Declan and I can play with Peppy in the yard. I kind of butted in here."

"It's okay," Vanessa said.

"That would be great," Luke said. "I need to scold my sister." He put an arm around Vanessa. He also needed to keep her from telling Angie the ugly truth about her husband.

"Declan," Angie said, "do you have a ball Peppy could play with?"

"Yeah!" Declan stuffed another cookie into his mouth and ran to the front room, returning seconds later with a tennis ball. "Come on!"

"Careful in the street," Vanessa called.

"I will be, Mom." Declan ran outside, followed closely by Angie and Peppy.

As soon as the trio were out of sight, Vanessa grabbed his hand. "You like her."

Of course, his sister recognized the truth. She'd always been able to read him. "I do," he said, "but she's not for me."

"Why not?"

"Lots of reasons. And don't try to shift the focus onto me. What happened today? Why didn't you eat?"

Vanessa sighed. "The truth is, we ran a little short of money. I didn't have enough for my kind of food, only Declan's, and he comes first."

"Your kind of food being fruits and vegetables?"

She nodded. "So much healthier. You should eat more of them yourself."

The irony of Vanessa preaching health while passing out from her own condition wasn't lost on Luke. He pulled out his wallet and extracted three twenties. "You know you only have to ask."

"No, it's okay, my check is coming in the next day or two."

"You need to eat now. You can pay me back." He pushed the money toward her. "Promise me you'll use it to buy food you're willing to eat."

"I promise." She leaned against him. "Thanks for bailing me out again. You're the best brother a girl could have."

"And you're the best sister, even if you're a pain in the neck sometimes." He hugged her.

As he went outside, Luke reminded himself that he needed to focus on his goals and get Vanessa into treatment. He couldn't let his interest in Angie derail that.

Helping Vanessa meant forgetting about Angie, and that was fine. Family came first.

Chapter Seven

This was going to work just fine.

Angie walked through the growing crowd of people on the town waterfront, Peppy at her side.

And only Peppy.

After the difficult day they'd had yesterday with Luke's sister, Luke had mentioned the Memorial Day parade and ceremony and invited her to come with him, but she'd declined. Said she had other plans.

Which was true. She planned to come downtown and walk around by herself, just her and Peppy, like they'd done last year. She'd see friends and enjoy the specials offered by the shops and food trucks, take in the fresh, summery bay air.

She would *not* stroll through the festivities at Luke's side, getting ever more attached to a man who would never be right for her.

The downtown streets were lined with people, some with lawn chairs, some sitting on the curb. From the other side of town, the sound of the high-school marching band drifted to them, stopping and starting in a last-minute, off-key rehearsal.

Clouds covered the sky, all but a few blue patches, and the air felt warm and close, even at ten o'clock. It was going to be a hot one, people kept saying as they greeted each other.

Angie waved at Brian and Elizabeth, who stood talking

with a group of friends. She'd had such a nice time at their place, and she'd half expected Elizabeth to speak with her about Luke. But apparently she was backing off the match-making. That was a good thing.

"Hello, Angie." The cool greeting pulled her from her thoughts.

Mrs. Ralston-Jones sat on a bench, fanning herself with an actual old-fashioned fan.

Angie wanted to pretend not to hear, but she forced herself to overcome it and smile at the older woman. "Hi, Priscilla," she said. "What do you think of this heat?" When in doubt, talk about the weather. That was something she'd learned from Oscar, one of his many lessons in the social graces that had proven genuinely helpful.

"It's just dreadful," Mrs. Ralston-Jones said. "Can you believe my air conditioning system isn't working?"

"Oh, no," Angie said. "I hope you found someone to fix it quickly."

"It's going to be three days," the woman said, fanning herself more vigorously. "I tried to get my old handyman, Luke Johnson, to work on it today, but he said he's busy."

Or maybe, since you dumped him before, he doesn't feel obligated to drop everything on a holiday and come solve your problems.

"I hope you get it worked out," Angie said and walked on. She was afraid that if she stayed, she'd say something that would reveal her negative feelings toward Mrs. Ralston-Jones. She had trouble liking a woman who seemed to specialize in rudeness. But she tried not to judge others. You never knew what a person was going through.

Besides, you shouldn't burn your bridges, especially with the wealthy and powerful. It was another lesson Oscar had taught her.

"Hey, Angie." It was Megan, Caleb's mom and Mrs. Ralston-Jones's daughter, whom she'd met that day at the school. They chatted for a few minutes, and Angie marveled at how different a mother and daughter could be. Megan seemed authentic and kind.

Angie congratulated herself internally. She'd barely thought about Luke during this morning, and that was so much healthier for her. She had a life, friends, goals. She didn't need to swoon over a man as if she were a lovesick middle schooler.

"Miss Angie! Peppy!" The boy's high voice rose above the sounds of the crowd, and then Declan rushed over. He greeted her and knelt to pet Peppy, obviously the main attraction. A moment later, Vanessa came up, breathing hard. "Hi, Angie," she said. "Listen, I wanted to thank you for helping yesterday. I'm embarrassed. I just forgot to eat."

From what Luke had said, it was more than that, but Angie wasn't going to push. "Are you feeling better?" she asked.

"Much. And Declan is loving the chocolate chip cookies you left at our place."

They followed the crowd to the small amphitheater on the waterfront, and a master of ceremonies came to the stage, dressed in full uniform. "Guard, advance," he said, and everyone quieted as a quadrant of soldiers from all branches of the military walked forward. They carried an open, casket-shaped box filled with flowers on their shoulders, as if they were pallbearers.

"Halt!" the master of ceremonies said.

The group stopped then set the flower casket down on a stand. They all saluted.

"Please rise for the singing of the national anthem," the master of ceremonies said.

Angie stood and felt suddenly foggy because…there was Luke. In uniform. Looking absolutely stunning. He hadn't been one of those carrying the flowers, but he was walking behind them up to the platform.

There was a good-size crowd, and they sang the national anthem with enthusiasm. The mayor said a few words, followed by a woman who'd lost three family members in three different wars.

And then Luke walked to the platform. He looked out at the crowd until everyone fell completely silent. Then he spoke. "The following men and women from this area lost their lives in the service of our country."

Luke read the names, clearly and slowly. At some of them, people murmured. At others, there was quiet crying. Angie saw people comforting one another and thought: this is a good thing, to honor and remember.

After Luke had gone through the whole alphabetized list of names, probably forty or fifty, he paused, but didn't sit down or dismiss the crowd. He cleared his throat and began to speak.

"I'd like to bring up another group of veterans who aren't always mentioned on Memorial Day. I'm talking about those who brought the war home with them and lost their lives because of that." He paused and looked around. "Twenty-two. That's how many veterans are estimated to die by suicide each day, and we need to do more for them."

There was a slight murmur, and then the crowd was silent.

Luke went on. "Before family members come up to choose a flower for their fallen soldiers, I'd like to conclude this part of our ceremony by reading a short list of names, vets who took their own lives. These families have agreed they'd like to honor their departed soldiers this way. If there are others, feel free to take a flower for them, too. Memorial Day is for all of our fallen."

Now there was a slight murmur in the crowd. Angie

couldn't tell whether it was pro or anti this twist on the day's usual events.

As Luke began to read names, Vanessa pulled a tissue out and wiped her eyes. She wasn't the only one. As the names of the veterans who'd died by suicide were read, a few sobs were heard from the crowd.

At the end of the list, he looked around. "And finally… Raymond H. Johnson, private first class, Vietnam." He cleared his throat. "My father."

There was an audible gasp from the crowd, and Vanessa started to cry.

Angie stood still for a moment, stunned. That Luke and Vanessa's father had taken his own life, and that Luke had had the courage to say that to a crowd of people, nearly took her breath away.

The master of ceremonies invited everyone who'd lost a family member to come get a flower and cast it into the bay.

Declan hugged his still sobbing mother. "It's okay, Mom," he said, patting her back. Angie was pretty sure he hadn't understood what his uncle had said nor why his mom was crying, but he was a sweet, kind little boy. He wanted to help.

"Let's get you to your brother," Angie said to Vanessa. That was probably the best way to comfort the woman who'd lost her father due to what was now recognized as PTSD.

They made their way to the front of the crowd. Luke was talking to other men and women in uniform, but when he saw Vanessa, he excused himself and strode over. "Sorry, Nessie," he said. "I should have told you I was going to do that."

"No, it's good," she said between sniffles. "It's just… I never felt like I could mourn him on Memorial Day because of how he died."

"And you shouldn't." Mrs. Ralston-Jones had pushed through the crowd and reached them just as Vanessa spoke.

Now she faced Luke, hands on hips. "Memorial Day is for heroes who died on the battlefield, not for those who took their own lives afterward."

Vanessa looked stricken, and Luke looked disgusted. Angie opened her mouth to defend what Luke had done, but a couple of older servicemen had overheard and came over. They wore civilian clothes, but their veteran status was obvious from the medals they wore. "Excuse me, ma'am," one said, taking off his cap, "but I lost a brother that way, and I can guarantee he wouldn't have taken his own life if he hadn't been drafted into that environment and seen what he saw."

"And I lost two close friends to suicide, after they'd come home from the Korean War," the other man said.

The two older men, along with Luke, made a solid wall of valor that even Mrs. Ralston-Jones couldn't breach. The medal count on those three chests was blinding.

The older woman turned away without saying anything more.

"Do you want to get a flower for Dad?" Luke asked, and Vanessa nodded.

"Declan?"

"Can I stay and play with Peppy?" There was a whiny tone in Declan's voice, and Angie realized the child had been under quite a strain. Just in the past two days, he'd seen his mother unconscious and watched her have an emotional meltdown he didn't understand.

"Would it be okay if I took Declan over to the playground with Peppy and me?" Angie asked Luke and Vanessa, quietly.

"Of course." Luke's eyes crinkled in a smile.

"That would be great. Thank you." Vanessa squeezed her hand.

And as Angie led Declan and Peppy toward the play area, as Mrs. Ralston-Jones's grandson, Caleb, rushed to join them,

Angie realized that she hadn't done what she'd planned to do at all.

Rather than getting her mind off Luke, she was thinking about him more than ever.

On Thursday evening, Luke was still thinking about that emotional Memorial Day service as he led Declan and Caleb out of the carriage house.

He'd given them a quick dinner—spaghetti, jarred sauce and ground meat he'd browned. The boys hadn't praised his cooking, of course, but they'd eaten big plates of food.

Caleb and Declan were getting to an age where feeding them was a challenge. Vanessa was always complaining about the expense. But Luke liked seeing Declan eat well because his own childhood had involved bouts with hunger. He never wanted Declan to experience that. Never wanted him to develop the type of eating problems his mother had.

Anyway, Luke had been working hard all day and planned to continue, so he ate like a horse himself.

There were no leftovers.

They headed toward an area of Angie's property where brush needed to be cleared before he could complete the fence. He gave the boys gloves and had them help him for fifteen minutes then decided that they'd learned enough for one day about hard work.

Besides, it was easier to get something done when you weren't supervising two eight-year-olds with more energy than sense.

"You boys can run around, but stay where you can see me." He'd learned from his sister that that was a better line than "stay where I can see you" because a kid would always claim he thought you could see him. This way, the responsibility lay with the child to stay in an adult's line of sight.

"We will," Declan promised, "but first, can we go get Peppy to come out and play?"

Luke frowned. Declan had been staying with him a lot this week, and he'd invited himself over to Angie's twice to play with Peppy. That was one of the things Luke had hoped to forestall by inviting Caleb over to play.

"I hafta read to her," Caleb said with a winning smile. "My teacher said I have to get my homework book read by tomorrow, and I read better when Peppy's there."

"Me, too," Declan said, backing up his friend.

"I'll walk over with you to ask," Luke compromised. "No begging and no banging on the door if Miss Angie doesn't answer."

As they walked—or rather, Luke walked and the boys ran zigzags, full of energy—the flowers planted in front of Angie's house sent their fragrance his way. It smelled sweet, almost as sweet as Angie herself.

Luke would have tapped on the door lightly in case Angie was busy or didn't want to answer. But Caleb and Declan pounded, causing Peppy to race to the picture window and stand on the back of what looked like a couch, barking.

Angie said something sharp and Peppy stopped, and then the door opened. Angie was sliding her phone into the back pocket of ripped, flared jeans that looked like something from the 1970s.

"The boys wanted to know—"

"Can we play with Peppy?" they both begged, interrupting.

She laughed. "Of course. She'll love that." She held the door open, and Peppy rushed out.

"I'm working on that brushy area in the northwest corner," Luke said as the boys rolled around with the delighted dog. "I'll keep an eye on them, make sure they're gentle with Peppy."

"That's fine," she said. "In fact, I'll come out and help."

Luke tried to stifle the surge of happiness he felt. "No need for that. It's itchy, messy work."

"All the more reason to get it done quickly." She reached for a light sweatshirt that hung on a row of hooks. "I'll just grab my gardening gloves and shoes, and I'll be fine."

Those supplies were located in a little shed at the back of the house. As she pulled them out, he said, "I'm sorry Declan keeps bugging you. I thought having Caleb over would cut back on that, but I may have just doubled it."

"It's fine," she said. "I love kids. Always wanted them."

"Is there a reason you never had any?" he asked, and then could have kicked himself. "Sorry. Not my business." He'd known a few couples who struggled with infertility. Asking about babies could trigger all kinds of painful emotions.

"It's fine. We didn't have kids because Oscar didn't want them. I had to respect that. Kids should never feel unwanted by a parent, and Oscar was just too busy with his work."

He was also busy having affairs, Luke thought.

They worked side by side, pulling out brambles, digging out roots. Luke tried to take on the heaviest labor himself, reminding her she didn't have to do it, but she worked energetically and waved off his suggestions that she take a break. "I was working on a grant application all day," she said. "Sitting. I need to move."

The trouble was, Luke liked watching her move. Liked working with her, chatting with her.

Make progress, he reminded himself. Make money. That was what this was all about. Vanessa wasn't doing well, and he wanted to get her into a treatment program as soon as possible.

He looked down toward the creek and saw Caleb and Declan sitting in front of Peppy. Caleb had a book and actually seemed to be reading from it. That was pretty amazing for a kid who struggled in school. "Look," he said. "Therapy dog at work."

Angie looked in the direction he was pointing and smiled. "I'm not even there to tell her what to do. She just knows."

"Seems like a great program for kids," he said. Then he took a risk and added, "I'm sorry you didn't get to have your own. You'd be a great mom."

"Thanks." She smiled at him. "It's a big regret, but at the same time, I wouldn't change my decision to marry Oscar. Even though I lost him too soon."

"That must have been rough," Luke said, feeling awkward. He was in the odd position of disliking Oscar, a man he'd barely met, based on the little he'd seen and heard about him. "Is that why you want to target your therapy dog work toward kids?"

"It is," she said slowly. "Although, after your comments on Memorial Day, I'm even more convinced we should expand to work with veterans. That twenty-two-per-day statistic was sobering. I'd like to help with that if I could."

"Makes sense." Luke tugged at a stubborn bush then set about digging it out.

Angie was a great person, wanting to help others the way she did. She must be in her midthirties, from something she'd said, but with her hair pulled back in a ponytail and funky vinyl clogs on her feet, she looked like a high-school student.

How could Oscar have cheated on a woman as great as Angie?

"Luke Johnson!" A bellowing voice pulled him back into the present. Mrs. Ralston-Jones was marching toward them. "Where is my grandson?"

Luke looked around and pointed at the creek, where the two boys seemed to be trying to make a boat for Peppy.

"He needs to get home and do his homework," she said. "His mother isn't nearly strict enough with him."

"He did spend a good while reading to Peppy," Angie said, her voice mild. "But I'll go get him. I don't want you to get your shoes any dirtier than they already are. They're Ferragamos, aren't they?"

"Yes, they are." Mrs. Ralston-Jones studied her slightly mud-splattered loafers and then picked her way back toward her Lexus. Angie ran over to get Caleb.

Luke sighed. He'd made a little progress on the project tonight, but not a lot. Meanwhile, his feelings toward Angie continued to grow. The more time he spent with her, the more he liked her. She was a genuinely good person.

But watching her talk with Mrs. Ralston-Jones, he saw two wealthy women. It reminded him: she's not for you.

Now, if he could only make himself believe it.

On Saturday morning, Angie put Peppy in her holder and then got in her car. She tried to start it and got nothing but a click-click-click. On her next try, she didn't even get that.

Great. What was she going to do now?

She had individual reading appointments with three kids today, meeting at the library. All three struggled in school, and their families had signed them up for the Saturday morning program. They looked forward to the reading time, had asked her last week if she was coming to the library. If she and Peppy didn't show up…

There was a knock on her car window, and she looked out to see Luke. "Doesn't sound good," he said. "I can help you jump it."

"Thank you," she said, truly grateful. Only…she checked the time. "I'm going to have to make a quick call. I'm going to miss Peppy's reading appointments." She hated it so much, disappointing the kids.

"Where are the appointments? I can take you."

"They're at the library."

"Perfect. I'd like to browse for some books."

"It could be almost two hours," she warned.

"Not a problem. I need to check out the lobby of one of the downtown buildings for a job I'll be doing next week. Let's go."

They drove through the neighborhood and out onto the road that led to downtown. They passed the grocery store, a couple of fast food places and the ancient gas station where old Joe Porter still insisted on hand pumping everyone's gas. Luke drove comfortably, braking at stop lights and letting the first oncoming car make a left before proceeding forward, a mannerly habit known as the Maryland left.

While they drove, he reassured her that he could help her jump her truck later this afternoon, and that he'd help out with rides if she needed to take her car to the shop.

"How did I get along without you?" she joked. But it was one of those jokes that was sort of serious. Luke was proving to be a very helpful guy to have around.

Nice to look at, too.

He smiled as if he could read her appreciation, all levels of it. "Tell me about your visits today. What will it be like?"

So she told him some stories of kids reading to dogs, funny and poignant. "You'll see, if you stick around for a little bit. But you have to stay out of sight because part of the trick is to let the child be alone with the animal."

"Don't kids ever get rough with Peppy?" He swung the truck into the library parking lot and pulled up into the shady section.

"Not so far. We do some training—of the kids—and then

some supervised visits. If anyone seems like they can't handle it, we stick with supervised. But it's not ideal, since the kids interpret any adult as passing judgment."

They walked into the library, Peppy prancing beside them, almost wiggling with eagerness.

"She knows she's working, doesn't she?" Luke sounded amazed.

"Yes, and she loves it."

"Peppy!" The ecstatic voice belonged to Mira, a cute seven-year-old. "I got our book all picked out. It's about a dog!"

Peppy wagged her long, feathered tail.

Angie waved to Mira's grandma. "Let's go over to our nook so Peppy can hear the story," Angie said.

"Just Peppy can listen." Mira sounded uneasy as Luke came up beside Angie.

"That's right. You two have the nook to yourselves." She handed Mira Peppy's leash.

Mira led Peppy into a corner of the children's section, lined with colorful pillows and cozy blankets. She spent some time getting her pillows and Peppy organized just right. Then she opened her book.

"I keep an eye on them, just in case there's any problem," Angie explained quietly to Luke. "But Peppy's a pro, and Mira is used to her. There shouldn't be any issues."

Angie stepped back to lean against the wall, Luke beside her. They watched as Mira read to Peppy in an animated way, pointing to pictures and words, asking the dog questions.

Mira's grandmother approached when Mira's half hour was almost up. "Would you look at that," she said. "I never see that girl smile with a book in her hands, except when she's reading to Peppy."

"Hopefully, she'll start to associate it all together. Reading and being happy."

Luke stayed to watch the start of the next therapy-dog appointment then went off to do the errand he'd mentioned. When he returned, Angie was just finishing up.

"Thank you so much for driving me and Peppy around today," she said as they walked back to his truck. "The kids would have been disappointed if we'd had to cancel."

"It's not a problem," he said as he opened the passenger door for her. "I like watching you work." He waited while she settled Peppy in the back seat, then held out a hand and helped her into the truck.

His hands were callused and big enough to engulf hers, and his touch made her catch her breath. She looked quickly into his eyes and saw that they'd darkened. So he felt it, too.

She didn't want to look away. Didn't want to let go of his hand.

She was playing with fire. She knew it, and it looked like he did, too.

She felt like a young girl with her first boyfriend, just starting to understand what love was. It was a feeling she needed to guard against. A better person would pull back, act cool and collected, build a little distance between them.

But she'd never gone through this phase of a relationship before. Men had been admiring her since she was young, but for the most superficial of reasons, and she'd had no feelings back toward them. Except with Oscar, but even with him, there was the baggage of how they'd met.

For the first time, she was interested in a man because they were compatible and because she found him attractive and admirable. It was a heady sensation.

She might enjoy it, sure, but she had to be careful. It would be easy to let this go out of control. And that would be a disaster.

Chapter Eight

On Saturday night, the first of June and just a week after Memorial Day weekend, Angie stood in line to board the Chesapeake Cruiser, a riverboat that tonight was hosting a dinner dance.

She wore one of her old formal dresses from her previous life—for that was how she'd come to think of her years with Oscar, another life. The people around her were his sort of people; in fact, she even saw a familiar face or two.

What was different was who was beside her: Peppy…and Luke.

How had this happened?

Luke looked sideways at her, and one corner of his mouth turned upward. "Pretty fancy," he said.

"It is." She met his eyes. "Thanks for coming with me."

They moved forward. A cool breeze from the bay made her shiver, and he grabbed hold of the wrap she'd tied loosely around the chain of her small purse. He lifted her hair and draped it around her shoulders.

When his fingers brushed her neck, she shivered again. This time, not from cold.

It was all about Luke. He was so tall and broad shoul-dered, literally standing above the other men waiting in line.

And she didn't need to be thinking about that. She adjusted her wrap and smiled at him in what she hoped was an impersonal way. "Thanks," she said. Then she deliberately turned and made small talk with the couple behind them. It was easy to do because, in addition to the weather to talk about, she had Peppy on a leash beside her. Everyone wanted to know why, of course.

That was good. She was getting attention for her program. That was the reason she was here. Not to enjoy Luke's gentle touch.

When there was a break in the conversation, she looked over to find him studying her. "You really are nervous about your presentation, aren't you?"

"I am." She picked up Peppy and cuddled the little dog close. "We'll get through it, though, won't we, girl? Because we're raising money for a good cause."

"You'll get through it fine." Luke put an arm around her shoulders and gave her a quick side hug that soothed her at the same time it made her heart rate quicken. His warmth, his strength, his very size, all of it felt comforting, like Luke would protect and take care of her.

And she shouldn't compare Luke to Oscar, but Oscar had been five-six to her five-nine. Luke was well over six feet, so the fact that she was wearing heels didn't faze him.

Although she suspected that Luke would be confident even if the woman he was with towered above him.

Plus, Luke's attention was solely on her, rather than on all the important people boarding the boat, talking and laughing around them. Oscar would have focused on seeing and being seen. That was what had made him such a success in the business world. He'd liked having her with him at some of his events, but her role had always been to look good and keep quiet.

Today, she was a part of the event, one of the speakers.

It was strange to be the center of attention, but because she believed in her cause, it was worth it.

They gave their names to the greeter and followed the crowd into the boat's main indoor area.

"Angie!" Mary Lido, the event's organizer and a social leader in the region, rushed over. "I'm so glad you're here. You're going to keep this event from being the stuffy thing it usually is."

"That's a lot of responsibility," Angie said, laughing. "Mary, this is Luke Johnson, who very kindly stepped in when my escort got sick."

"Pleased to meet you," Mary said. She gave Luke a frank appraisal. "Just between us, I think you're better off with the replacement date."

Angie laughed, her face heating. She noticed that Luke's face had flushed a little, too. For the first time, she realized that focusing on his good looks was a sort of objectification, something she'd always disliked when it was targeted at her. She needed to work on that. "You may be right," she said to Mary. "Luke's a good person and a supportive friend."

It was true. She'd been out on her deck, talking to Luke about the project, when she'd gotten the call that her planned escort, an old friend of Oscar's, wasn't feeling well. She'd spoken to Peppy aloud, as she often did: "What are we going to do now, girl? We can't go into that crowd alone!"

Luke had overheard, and she'd explained the situation and then impulsively asked if he'd be able to go, last minute. He'd agreed without any hesitation.

And here he was, dressed in a dark suit she snobbishly hadn't expected a handyman to have. It wasn't the latest style or a summer one—a lot of the men wore paler color jackets or even seersucker—but then, a lot of the men here were seventy and up. Luke, with his tall, slim build and dark good looks, had drawn the eye of a number of the ladies.

He drew her eye, too, continuously. But she needed to focus: on his character traits and not his looks, and on her own goals for this event. "So how's this going to work?" she asked Mary. "When is my presentation?"

"After dinner," Mary said. "We're putting you as the last of the three presentations because we figure you and Peppy can keep people's attention even if they're full or sleepy or want to dance."

"In other words, the toughest spot," she said, smiling to show she wasn't mad about it. Truly, she was just glad to get an opportunity to seek funders and donations for her dog reading program.

"Yes, kind of," Mary said. "But people tend to remember the last speaker best, so you just may get more support in this time slot." She smiled at them. "Dinner's not for another half hour, so grab a drink, walk around, enjoy yourselves."

"We will," Angie said to Mary's back, as the woman was called away to deal with something in the kitchen.

She looked up at Luke. "Want something to drink?"

"No, thanks. I'm not much of a drinker. But I can get you something."

"I'm fine with a soda at dinner. Let's walk around."

"I'd like to go upstairs, see the water," he said. "I don't get a whole lot of opportunities to be on a boat."

"Sounds good to me." She picked up Peppy, and they headed outside and up the steps.

On the top deck, people clustered along the railing, looking out at the water as the boat slowly chugged away from the dock. It was a happy, chatty crowd. Anything planned by Mary Lido was well thought out, with a clear dress code and everything organized to make sure people had a good time.

Some of the attendees sat down on the rows of benches. A couple of waiters circulated with trays of appetizers.

The breeze Angie had felt before was stronger now as they entered the open water. The boat swayed and rocked a little. The sound of the engine was low in the background, behind people's conversation and laughter.

"What a cute dog!" a woman said, turning from the cluster of women she'd been speaking to.

"Yes, but why is there a dog on board where food is served?" another woman asked.

"She's part of an after-dinner presentation," Angie explained. "She's a therapy dog."

The woman who'd initially spoken was petting Peppy, who was being her usual charming self, winning people over.

The woman who'd complained frowned. "I just don't understand how my generation was able to get through life just fine without dogs and disability accommodations and perfectly politically correct language, when folks today can't do without them."

"Young people today are needy," a white-haired gentleman said.

"Exactly!" The woman who'd complained smiled up at the man. "We didn't need therapy dogs or any kind of therapy, for that matter."

Then they both looked at Angie and Luke, as if expecting them to argue.

Luke smiled back at them, but he was irritated; Angie could tell from the way a muscle jumped in his cheek. "I don't know about that," he said, his voice mild. "Plenty of people in my parents' generation would have benefited from therapy. My own folks included."

Angie nodded. "Mine, too. But Peppy isn't just any therapy dog. She's helping kids learn to read."

"How can that be?" It was the man speaking, but both he and the woman with him looked incredulous.

"You'll have to stay for the presentation to see." She smiled at them. "It was nice to meet you. We're going to go check out the views before dinner."

"This way," Luke said quietly and took her arm. He guided her toward a less crowded section of the deck.

A seagull landed on the boat's railing, and Peppy barked, startled, then cowered when the bird cawed. Several of the people around them looked disapprovingly, including the couple they'd spoken to. Most of them laughed.

Luke laughed, too. "Peppy isn't exactly aggressive, is she?"

"No, she's not." Impulsively, she took his hand and squeezed it. "Thank you for coming with me. I'm guessing this isn't your scene."

"It's not," he agreed, "but I'd be a fool to turn down a pretty night and a pretty lady."

Her cheeks heated. She wasn't sure where they stood. That remark had made the evening sound like a date.

They walked to the railing of the small back deck. The sun was a gold ball amongst scattered light clouds, and the water sparkled a dark gray-blue. Seabirds swooped and called. The boat's motor had gone quiet, and the sound of the water was audible, lapping against the boat.

"Ever been on one of these before?" she asked Luke.

"No. Well, as a teenager I worked a couple of cruises when a local catering company needed a few extra people. But it wasn't for me." His mouth quirked up in a rueful smile. "Keeping track of people's orders and making sure not to spill dinner plates in someone's lap definitely isn't my strong suit. Especially when you're also supposed to act subservient and nice."

Angie tried to imagine Luke waiting tables. It didn't quite fit. "It doesn't seem like the kind of work you'd enjoy."

"I didn't know how to get along with all the wealthy customers. I resented them. It seemed like they had everything and I had nothing. Typical self-centered attitude of a teenager."

"You seem to do fine now, working with the wealthy." She thought of Mrs. Ralston-Jones. "Most of them, at least."

He smiled, looking out onto the water. "Working in their homes all these years, I've seen their feet of clay. How about you? Been on cruises before, I assume?"

She nodded. "Did them with Oscar some. I liked being on a boat better than in some big overcrowded ballroom in the city."

"But…it sounds like you didn't come from wealth."

Angie sucked in a breath and hesitated. Should she tell him the true story of her background and how she'd met Oscar?

Maybe at some point, but not now, she decided. She had to keep herself together for her presentation. "I grew up middle class," she said, electing to focus on her younger years and be vague. "Certainly not attending events like this. Oh, look, I think they're calling people down to dinner."

As they finished their delicious dinner of crab cakes and steamed shrimp, Luke couldn't keep his eyes off Angie. She was just so pretty, whether she was talking to the ninety-something couple on her right or checking to make sure Peppy had a bowl of water under the table. That was why he noticed when she started to get nervous.

He cast about mentally for some way to help her but was at a loss until a woman beside him provided an opportunity, asking him about his connection to the event and to literacy.

"My connection is Angie," he said, nodding sideways toward her. "But also, I struggled with it. I didn't learn to read until I was in fifth grade, not really. I had a hard time, so I'm aware of how important it is that kids get a good start with books and reading."

That got a discussion going at the table, people's experiences with reading. Calmed Angie's nerves, he could tell, and she jumped in and talked some about the dog program, and people were interested.

But when the after-dinner presentations started, she tensed up again. Her knee was bouncing up and down, and she twisted her cloth napkin in her hands, restlessly.

He put a hand on hers, stilling them. "Why don't you give your presentation to Peppy?" he suggested.

She laughed at the idea. "What do you mean?"

"Just talk to Peppy. She's going to be on the stage with you, right? Or if you'd like, I'll hold her here. Just look at her and talk to her."

She leaned over and kissed his cheek. "You're brilliant," she said. "I was going to have her beside me, but if I can look at her, I'll be calmer." And then the second speaker was done, and the woman they'd met earlier was introducing her.

And Luke was trying to calm his heart rate, which had shot up when she'd kissed him. Man, he was in trouble. He needed to get a grip.

"Will you come up front with me and hold Peppy?" she asked.

He hadn't bargained for that, but for Angie, he was realizing, he'd do just about anything. "Uh…sure."

She handed him the little dog, grabbed her notes and led the way toward the stage. She pulled over a chair so he could sit in the front row then proceeded up the steps and walked to the microphone.

"I'm a little nervous," she said in that low, smoky voice that brought everyone in the room instantly to attention. Especially the men, Luke observed. "So I'm going to give my presentation to Peppy, here."

She adjusted the technology, moved to her first slide and started talking…to Peppy.

And it worked. It took people a few minutes to figure out that she was illustrating the very thing she wanted them to fund. But when they got it, they loved it.

Luke hadn't expected to be up front and the center of attention, but after a minute he stopped sweating. Peppy was all anyone was watching. When Angie's presentation ended, she got more applause than the other two presenters put together.

He said as much to her as they left the stage. "Let's hope it turns into donations," she responded.

The band kicked in, and people moved onto the dance floor. Of course, Angie was swamped with offers from gentlemen old and young. Luke turned down a couple of requests to dance himself, citing his need to stay with Peppy.

He drank a soda, alone at the table, watching Angie. She was smiling and pleasant to everyone, but something made him think she wasn't comfortable, didn't love this world.

Which, he reminded himself, didn't matter. The fact that she'd kissed his cheek didn't matter. It was friendship, and it could never be anything more.

He looked around the room, wondering how many of these wealthy people had secrets to hide. Like Oscar, her husband, hiding his affair with Luke's sister.

Angie looked at him over the shoulder of some particularly enthusiastic dance partner whose hands were sliding a little too low past her waist. She gave him a creased-forehead smile. "Save me," she mouthed.

Instantly, he was on his feet. He handed Peppy to a woman

who'd admired the dog before and strode over to where Angie was tugging away from the older guy who, Luke realized now, reeked of whiskey. "Excuse me," he said, and pulled Angie into his arms.

"Hey!" the guy said, too loud, and then a woman, presumably his wife, grabbed his arm and pulled him off the dance floor, scolding him the whole time.

Luke wasn't much of a dancer, but it was a slow song. He just pulled Angie close—not too close, like her previous partner had—and swayed with the music.

She felt good in his arms, slender but strong. Her hair, cascading down her back, was as soft as he'd imagined it to be.

She looked up at him. "Thanks for rescuing me," she said.

"My pleasure." He wasn't lying. The way she felt, her gratitude, the feeling of protecting her, all of it made his chest swell with pride. Not to mention the pride he felt in dancing with the prettiest woman in the room.

You're not her boyfriend, he reminded himself. *You're just a last-minute stand-in.*

When the song ended, he let go of her and stepped back. His arms felt empty.

Someone else came up and wanted to dance with her, and he stepped away. "I'll get Peppy," he said. "I'll take her upstairs, where we were before."

"Thank you. I mean it." Her eyes were warm on him, and just like that, he felt ten feet tall again.

He retrieved Peppy and carried her, stopping to talk with various people along the way. Having the dog with him, it was easy. He found himself telling several people about his struggles with reading and reinforcing Angie's point that reading to an animal could have helped with the tension reading always evoked in him as a child.

After a few minutes, he walked to the back deck and sat

down. Peppy flopped to her side, clearly exhausted by the evening's proceedings.

Maybe Angie would come up here and sit with him. Maybe, in the starlight, with the moon making a silvery path across the water, he'd even kiss her.

Maybe she'd even let him.

She. Is. Not. For. You.

He forced himself to remember Vanessa's pallor, her passing out, the way she'd been more and more unable to care for Declan. Taking care of her was Luke's first responsibility.

Getting hooked up with a rich woman was not. In fact, it was irresponsible. No way could he support Angie in the style she was used to, even if that opportunity presented itself.

No. He had to get out of here. He took Peppy back into the crowd on the front deck and forced himself to make nice with people and chat with them. Angie came up and, not seeing him, headed for the back deck.

Everything in him longed to go back there, hold her, congratulate her on a job well done, celebrate with her.

But he didn't do it. He stayed in the crowd, and after the boat docked, he kept things light on the drive home.

And tossed and turned all night, thinking about her.

Chapter Nine

Angie was *not* going to Luke's church today. She wasn't going to see him at all. As soon as TV church was over, she was going downtown—alone—and strolling through the Waterfront Festival.

Last night, the boat cruise had been way too intense. She'd been nervous about her presentation, and it had caused her to let down her guard and experience some very disturbing feelings about Luke.

She liked him. Way too much.

Luke seemed like one of the truly good guys, of whom there were few left in the world. He worked hard and used his skills to help people. He was humble about his background, both what he'd overcome and his time in combat overseas. He helped his sister and nephew. Probably financially, but more importantly, by being there for them, stepping in to make sure that Vanessa was okay and that Declan had a good childhood.

And then there was the fact that he was so handsome, with his dark hair and warm brown eyes and strong arms. She was a sucker for strong arms.

Outside, she heard a truck door slamming then Declan's shouts. Luke and Declan were back from church already. She needed to stop thinking about Luke, needed to avoid him.

She changed into a sundress and comfortable sandals. Peppy jumped and yipped, obviously hoping to go along. Angie knelt and petted her sweet girl's soft fur. "You can't come this time, but Mommy will be home soon."

Peppy understood enough to tilt her head with that heartbreaking, manipulative mixture of sadness about being left behind and hope that Angie would change her mind.

Angie gave her dog one last pat then slipped over to the window and looked out. Luke and Declan appeared to have gone inside the carriage house.

Time to make her escape.

She grabbed her purse and set out toward downtown, walking quickly until she was out of sight of the house. Then she settled down to enjoy the rest of the half-mile walk.

It was a beautiful June Sunday, and the town was alive with people gardening, grilling or relaxing on the front porches for which Chesapeake Corners was known. Kids rode bikes or played hopscotch or tossed a football. Dogs barked from behind picket fences, and wild roses emitted their sweet scents into the breeze.

As she got closer to downtown and the festival, the noise level rose. A band played classic beach songs, guitar and drums and sax, from a temporary stage, and an elaborate bouncy structure echoed with kids' voices. From the bay, an announcer proclaimed the winners of the first round of a fishing contest.

Angie headed for the line of booths selling all sorts of goods, from candles to fudge to dog novelties. At the latter, she picked up a new kerchief and a couple of biscuits for Peppy.

"Angie!" It was Gabby, Caleb and Declan's teacher. The woman hugged her as if they were old friends. Apparently, she'd never met a stranger. "Girl, you've got to try the fudge from Chesapeake Chocolate. It is to die for." She opened a white paper bag and offered Angie a piece.

Angie demurred at first, but Gabby waved the bag under her nose. When she smelled the chocolate, she gave in. "Just one piece," she agreed, and Gabby handed her a square of fudge, complete with nuts and marshmallows.

Angie tasted it, and her eyes widened at the creamy, chocolaty goodness. "Wow. Thank you. This is amazing."

"Told you so," Gabby said. "How's the therapy-dog work going?"

"It's good." Angie told Gabby a little about her gig at the library and the fundraising work she'd been doing. "If all goes well, I can start training another dog soon. I want to try having some dogs that various people can work with and that can be a resource for existing therapy teams."

"That's so cool," Gabby said. "If you need a teacher consultant, I'm your woman." She took a swig of coffee. "Hey, how's Luke? I heard he's living on your property. And that you're spending a lot of time together."

Angie frowned. Just what she was trying to avoid thinking about. "If you don't mind my asking, how did you hear that?"

"Declan," Gabby explained. "You wouldn't believe the stuff kids tell their teachers and classmates. But don't worry, I'll keep it to myself."

"Nothing to hide," Angie said quickly. "He's just living there while he does some work for me."

"No need to explain." Gabby shrugged and wiped her fingers on a napkin. "Believe me, I have no time for gossip and no interest in it, either. It's great to see you, Angie. Let's get coffee sometime."

"I'd like that."

She walked on. This was good. This was fun. She didn't

need to orient her life around Luke Johnson, shouldn't. She had a perfectly fine life as a single.

A widow, she reminded herself. She'd tried marriage, even succeeded at it, which was a little surprising given her background. She'd worked hard to be a good wife to Oscar, and he'd seemed happy. He'd grown more and more affectionate toward the end of his life, talking about how good she was to him and how happy she'd made him in his later years.

Thinking about Oscar gave her a warm feeling, tinged with regret. He'd died too soon. She'd thought they would spend his retirement years traveling, going to the art museums he loved and entertaining his friends. But he'd never had the chance to retire.

No one knew how much time they'd be given. Maybe the fact that it was Sunday, or that she'd read the Bible and watched a church service online, made her reflective. She wondered whether she'd done all she wanted and needed to do with her life.

Her biggest regret was that she didn't have children. She'd always wanted them. Wanted to create a loving family that would be a true port in a storm, rather than a place to escape from, like her own family of origin had been.

But she knew, better than a lot of people, that you didn't always get what you wanted. Children were a hard no for Oscar, and she'd understood that going in. She'd been able to live with it, even though her regret about it had grown as she'd passed the age of easy childbearing.

Now Luke…*he* seemed like he'd love to have kids, though he was older too and probably wouldn't become a father at this point. Of course, men could become dads late in life, as was evident by the recent spate of famous seventy-something men with babies.

But they all had young wives. She'd been that to Oscar, but

she was outgrowing that category. At thirty-seven, she wasn't trophy-wife material and couldn't have kids much longer.

Luke could, though, and he probably should. He was good-looking, kind and hardworking. Not wealthy, but he could easily attract a younger woman on the basis of his looks and personality, should he decide he wanted kids.

Something made her look down the street, a weird kind of radar, and there he was, the man she'd been thinking about even though she didn't intend to. He was walking alongside his sister, Vanessa, and Declan. What was this new awareness she had in relation to Luke, that she sensed his presence even before she saw him?

Feeling suddenly shy, she ducked into one of the booths and studied the varied soaps and lotions for sale, staying so long that she finally bought several items just to support the soap maker whose tent she'd co-opted.

Surely Luke and his family would have moved on to another part of the festival by now. She couldn't imagine Declan enjoying the home goods that dominated this row of booths.

Inhaling the sweet fragrance of honeysuckle and lavender from the small bag, she walked out of the soap booth... and almost ran into Luke.

She took a big step back. "Hi!" she said, certain that her disconcerted feeling was obvious. "Where are Vanessa and Declan?"

"So you did see us," he said, lifting an eyebrow. "Are you avoiding me?"

"No!" She stepped off the sidewalk to get out of the way of people walking by, and Luke stepped with her. They stood in the shade of a big oak tree. "Well, maybe I was avoiding you guys a little."

"Can I ask why?" His brown eyes were concerned. "I hope I didn't do anything to offend you last night."

The opposite. I enjoyed last night too much.

She couldn't admit that. But maybe it was the warm Sunday or the emotional thoughts she'd been having about Oscar and kids and life, but she impulsively blurted out the truth. "There's something building between us. I don't know if you feel it, but I do, and I can't let that happen."

There. It was out there.

He tilted his head to one side, studying her. Then he turned toward the bay, gesturing for her to walk beside him. "I'm not saying you're wrong," he said once they were walking. "But from your angle, why can't we let it happen?"

She heaved a sigh. "I'm not who you think I am."

"What do you mean?" His question was sharp, and so was his sideways glance at her.

Should she tell him?

She'd spent a lot of time keeping her past a secret. But with Luke, she hated the deception. "It's sort of an ugly story," she said.

They passed a group of sidewalk chalk artists, surrounded by a curious crowd, and continued on toward the water. "Does your story have a happy ending?" he asked.

Did it? "I really don't know," she said. "Not yet, anyway."

They walked together quietly for a few minutes, strolling to an outlook over the bay and leaning on the railing, side by side. "I love to watch the sailboats," she said.

"Do you sail?"

She laughed. "No, not really. Oscar and I went out boating sometimes, but someone else was in charge of making sure we didn't capsize."

"The most boating I ever did was in an old leaky rowboat," he said. "Our backgrounds are pretty different."

"I might have mentioned this before, but I didn't grow up

wealthy," she said quickly. "The only boats in my life were after I married Oscar."

He nodded, studied her. "Do you like ice cream?" he asked abruptly.

"Well...of course. Who doesn't?"

"Let's get cones from Wagner's." Wagner's was the non-chain ice cream store at the edge of the boardwalk.

"Okay, sure." She felt relieved to be off the hook about telling him more about her past, and also a little let down. He must not want to hear about it.

But ice cream was always good. The fudge Gabby had given her had whetted her taste for chocolate, so she ordered a double cone of it. Luke got butter pecan, and by now, she knew enough to let him pay for her cone. They headed to the outdoor deck, overlooking the bay where boats were already lining up for the afternoon boat parade.

"So if you didn't grow up wealthy," he said when they were nearly done eating, "how'd you meet a man like Oscar?"

Here it came. Her stomach tightened. "You really want to know?"

"I do, if you don't mind talking about it."

Okay then. She took a deep breath. "So... I wasn't always the person you see right now. Oscar, well, he kind of saved me."

He looked at her then out toward the water, giving her space. A family that had been eating lunch on the other side of the deck headed inside, and they had the area to themselves.

"He saved you from what? Your stepdad?"

"Not directly. I mean, my stepdad wasn't...the greatest. I needed to get out, and I did."

"Your mom?" he asked.

Angie shook her head. "She was so in love with him that she couldn't admit he had a bad side. So I left."

"How old were you?"

"I was just sixteen. Making decisions like a sixteen-year-old, meaning, I didn't think them through real well."

"Understandable at that age." He picked up her hand and squeezed it, his forehead wrinkled, his eyes warm and concerned. "Then what happened?"

She didn't want to go into detail, even in her own mind. "I had a couple of bad years," she said. "And then I got rescued."

"By Oscar."

"No. Not yet." She swallowed hard. "I was actually rescued, the first time, by…" She swallowed. "By the owner of an exotic dance club."

Now his focus was entirely on her, but she couldn't read his face. Was he scornful? Pitying? Had he ever been in such a place? Did he know what they were like?

Even that much of a memory made her feel sick inside. She pulled her hand from his and wrapped both arms around her middle.

"I felt like there was no choice," she said, defending herself even though he hadn't questioned her decision. "It was either the streets and the abuse there, or home and the abuse there, or…dancing. I made enough money to pay for my own little apartment. Buy bread and lunch meat. It was better than it had been before."

"I thought…" He paused.

"What?"

"I thought people who worked in places like that did pretty well, financially."

She shook her head rapidly. "Only if they did more than dance." But dancing had been enough. Degrading enough, humiliating enough. She'd seen things that had stolen the last bit of her innocence away.

She glanced sideways at him, forecasting what his reaction might be. Christian kindness, probably. And a cooling off of any romantic feelings he might have had before learning the truth about her.

He was too good and upright and Christian for her. She'd known it all along. It was just as well he heard the truth about the past now, before she got even more drawn to him.

She sighed and crumpled up her napkin and tossed it into the trash. And waited for him to make an excuse to get away from her, as far as possible, as fast as possible.

Luke tried not to stare at Angie, across the table from him on the now deserted deck of the ice cream shop.

Her sweet face was so at odds with the tale she was telling him. Yet the pain in her eyes confirmed that it was all true.

"I can't understand how you got through all that," he said finally. "I'm really sorry."

She lifted one shoulder in a shrug. "It turned out okay."

Had it, though? She was obviously still affected by what she'd seen and done. How could she not be? He found that he wanted to talk to her about it, wanted to help her process what she probably didn't share with many people. But it was hard to know how to start. "What was it like for you?" he asked finally.

She tilted her head to one side, a strand of hair blowing across her face in the increasing breeze. She pushed it back. "You're not the type of guy who thinks exotic dancing is a fun thing to hear about, are you?"

"No!" He shook his head. "No way. It's…not for me." Having been in the service, he'd seen and heard about so-called gentlemen's clubs, but he'd never found their concept compelling. How could any connections made there not be forced and fake?

She studied his face skeptically. Maybe she had tried to

tell others her story before and discovered it evoked interest of the wrong kind.

"The truth is," he said, fumbling for the right words, "I'm not much for going out, whether to drink or look at girls or… whatever. When other guys in my unit were out partying, that was when I got more into reading. I literally read *War and Peace* in a war zone."

She gave a quick, startled laugh. "You're kidding."

"Not kidding. It started out as a joke. Some of the guys gave me a copy that had come in a donation box. But I got into it." He was glad he'd managed to make her smile. He sensed, though, that there was more she needed to get off her chest. And he *was* curious. Not in a weird way, but because, for better or worse, he cared about her. "When I asked what it was like for you, I just wanted to know you better. Was it completely miserable, or did you make friends with the other dancers? That kind of thing."

"Nobody asks questions like that," she said slowly. "I mean, hardly anyone knows I did it, but even Oscar didn't wonder what my life was actually like back then." She zipped up her jacket, shivering a little. "Most of the girls were like me. They weren't born wanting a job like that. It was just a combination of having the looks men like and circumstances."

Luke blew out a breath. Her casual assessment—"the looks men like"—took him aback a little.

She studied his face. "What?"

"It's just… *I* like the way you look. Does that make me a jerk, like the men in your audience?"

She raised an eyebrow. "Depends on how you act about it."

"I'll try to act respectful, but call me on it if I'm annoying."

"Will do. And I don't mean to be stuck-up about how I

look. Lots of other women are a lot prettier than me. It's just the long red hair. The thing that got me teased in school turned out to be an asset. Sort of."

It was more than the long red hair, but he liked that she underplayed how pretty she was, maybe wasn't even aware of it.

The wind blew his napkin off the table, and he lunged to grab it. He tossed it in the trash then sat back down. "Tell me more," he said. "If you feel like it."

She shrugged. "In some ways, the camaraderie was the best thing. We girls had each other's backs." She smiled. "My apartment was close to the club, and sometimes a couple of the girls would come over after the show. We'd put on our comfy clothes and watch old movies and eat way too much ice cream."

"Sounds fun," he said. It was just so normal of an activity. He could picture Angie enjoying it. "You said that was the best thing. What was the worst?"

She didn't hesitate. "What it made me think about men. I saw their worst side."

Luke thought of the way his army buddies had talked about women after going to the men's clubs. "Yeah, I guess you did." He was quiet for a minute, not sure what to say.

"Everyone wasn't awful." She looked down at the picnic table, picking at a sliver of wood. "The owner of the club was a decent guy. I mean, for the business he was in. Girls actually wanted to work there because he left them alone and offered some protection from customers."

Luke really, really hated that "some." He also hated that a men's club like that was a refuge. That meant her life before the club had been worse.

He couldn't believe he'd thought she was privileged and out of touch. Her life had been anything but easy. Until she met her husband, apparently. "How did you meet Oscar?" he asked. "Or is that one too many questions? You don't have to tell me anything." He shouldn't have asked it, not when he knew something she didn't about Oscar and his sister.

"It's okay. I met Oscar at the club." She flushed. "I know, I know, I disparaged our customers. But Oscar was there with some business acquaintances. He wasn't a regular or anything."

Her defense of the man twisted something in Luke's gut.

"One of the guys in his group got too handsy," she continued, "and Oscar stopped him. At that point, the original owner had sold the club, and things were going downhill. I was too upset to work anymore that night, so Oscar and I spent the evening together."

Luke was guessing Oscar had been happy to spend the evening with her. Had maybe even helped her out with that goal in mind.

She seemed to read his attitude in his eyes. "No, really. We just talked. He took me out and bought me food, asked me about myself, asked if he could see me again. He was so much nicer than anyone else had ever been to me." She was looking down at the floor now.

He started to reach for her and then pulled his hand back. "I'm not judging," he said, trying to make that be true. "It sounds like he was being a decent guy."

"He was." She nodded as if convincing herself. "He kept calling. He took me out to nice places. He didn't rush into anything. We got closer, and…" She smiled. "When he asked me to marry him, it was the most amazing thing. A girl like me, mocked in school, a dropout, being able to wear nice clothes and go nice places."

"I get that." He remembered the first time his commanding officer had taken him and a buddy to a nice steakhouse. He hadn't known how to act, what to order—had embarrassed himself by mispronouncing *filet mignon*—but it had felt amazing to be there. Like he was a different person.

"We're closing." A man in a white apron stuck his head out the back door. "You're welcome to sit there, but if you want any more food, now's the time."

"Thanks," Luke said distractedly. Then to Angie: "Do you want something to drink or anything?"

"No. The ice cream was great."

The worker went back inside. When Luke looked around, he realized the whole festival was closing down. A couple of people walked by quickly, carrying shopping bags. The vendors who hadn't already shut down were in the process of putting away their merchandise and securing their booths. The music that had been distant background noise had stopped.

Angie stood. "Any more questions before we go?"

There was one, but he didn't know exactly how to ask it. Luke stood then looked at her. She was looking up at him, her face clear, her shoulders relaxed. Talking about her past had given her some kind of relief, it seemed.

"Was the marriage a good one?" he asked.

She gave him a funny look. "Yes! I mean, so much better than my mom and stepdad had, or any of the other relationships I'd seen."

Her answer tugged at him. She had such low expectations. But given what she'd been through, that was understandable.

"Oscar was great," she said firmly. "He was a wonderful husband."

"Good," he said. He definitely couldn't tell her that Oscar had cheated with Vanessa. What would that do to someone already so disillusioned about men?

And yet…he felt such a warm protective feeling. He wanted to pull her into his arms and comfort her. Take care of her.

Was it possible he could know about Oscar and Vanessa, keep it from Angie and still get closer to her?

He knew it was his hormones talking. But she was so pretty and vulnerable. He wanted to be the one to treat her well. He wanted to be the one to be true to her.

Lightning flashed across the sky, followed by a loud boom of thunder. Angie gave a little shriek.

"We'd better get home, or to shelter," he said. "Come on, let's take a shortcut through the park."

They set out, walking fast. When the first drops of rain hit, they both started to run.

And then the skies opened up and it poured.

"Over here," Luke said, grabbing her hand and tugging her toward a gazebo that was nestled at the edge of the park.

The rain blew wildly, and the only moderately dry spot was the very center of the gazebo. Around them, rain fell in sheets. Lightning crashed and thunder reverberated. When Luke tucked her into the curve of his arm, she didn't object, but snuggled in.

"It'll blow by quickly," he said, looking out at the sky. He honestly had no idea if that was true, but he felt the need to be reassuring.

She giggled. "I haven't been caught in the rain in a long time," she said. "And hey…thanks for listening to my whole sordid story and still being nice."

He looked down at her. Her red hair was plastered against her bare, wet arms. She must not wear much makeup, because she didn't have streaks of mascara running down her face like he'd seen on a few other women, Vanessa in particular. "Seems to me that your past isn't your fault," he said.

She shrugged and started wringing water out of her sweatshirt. He liked that she wasn't picky about her clothes.

He liked so much about her. And wow, was he having urges to take that liking further.

But, especially toward someone with her background, he didn't want to be one of *those* men.

Besides, she'd said something about how they couldn't let it build. She was right; there were reasons from his angle, too.

Here in their own little world, though, with rain pouring around them, making the rest of the park virtually invisible, those reasons seemed a whole lot less relevant.

He looked down at her. She was looking up at him. There was something almost speculative in her eyes.

He sucked in a breath and touched her lips with the tip of one finger. Soft and full. Just like he'd imagined.

"What are you thinking?" she asked.

"I'm thinking I want to kiss you," he said.

She looked at him steadily for a moment. "Then why don't you do it?"

It was all the encouragement he needed. He lowered his lips to hers.

Chapter Ten

When Luke kissed Angie, she shivered, a deep shiver from the inside of her. This kiss was like nothing she'd ever experienced before. As if this were her first kiss.

"You're cold," he murmured against her lips and pulled her closer.

"You're…not." His broad chest felt like a heat source, his arms around her protecting her from the little needles of rain that attacked with each gust.

She felt him smile. "Like I mentioned before, I tend to run hot," he said, and she looked into his eyes. There was a knowing there, an awareness. What they felt for each other wasn't just a passing fancy and wouldn't dissipate with one little kiss.

He watched her and seemed to see her come to that realization. He scooped his hands into her hair, drawing her closer, ever closer. His arms were slick with rain. She touched his neck, his face. Felt the slight stubble of his beard. His eyes, looking down at her, were warm, caring.

When he kissed her again, it was deeper, and she sighed and relaxed against him. Something about his embrace made her feel…peaceful. Like she'd come home. He was just so stable and strong, like a rock, like a fortress.

He was so different from Oscar.

The thought of her late husband brought a flash of uneasiness. Why was she comparing? Why, when Luke was nothing like Oscar? Although Oscar had been a good man, and she'd loved him, Luke was in a whole different league. For one thing, he was a strong Christian, while Oscar had lapsed from his faith. For another...there was the way she and Oscar had met. Although she'd downplayed it to Luke, she'd always been a little ashamed before Oscar because he'd seen her dancing at the club, in front of other men. He hadn't ever said anything to put her down for that, and yet the knowledge had created the slightest wedge between them.

Luke lifted his head, studied her face and stepped back. Around them, the rain slackened a little. "Don't overthink this," he said. But when he pulled her close again, it was more of a warm and gentle embrace, not an intense kiss.

She wanted more kissing, but she knew it would be unwise. So she leaned her cheek against his chest and listened to the strong, steady beat of his heart. They stayed that way for long moments, until the rain had lightened enough for them to jog home, laughing, hand in hand.

Luke was still reliving that spectacular kiss the entire next day.

Fortunately, Vanessa had invited him over for dinner. He needed to think about something else, get some perspective. So after he'd cooled off from a day of outdoor work, showered and drunk a big jug of iced tea, Luke climbed in his truck and headed toward his sister's house.

He tried to focus on the road, the warm air coming through his open window, the smooth jazz playing on the radio. He had a goal: to ask his sister more about her relationship with Oscar. Maybe it hadn't been very serious. Maybe it had been brief and not something he needed to disclose to

Angie. Maybe it was just a small indiscretion that wouldn't bother Angie too much if it came to light.

Somehow, though, he knew that whatever it had been would bother her. Despite her background, she'd put her faith in Oscar. Having seen the worst in men, she'd still found a way to trust one of them.

And the man had betrayed her trust. Not to mention that he'd taken advantage of Luke's sister. If Oscar had been standing in front of him right now, Luke would have strong words to say to him.

But Oscar was gone, and maybe Luke could let the past be the past. Maybe it didn't matter what Angie's late husband had done long ago.

Because kissing Angie had changed everything.

Not just kissing her. Hearing her story. Understanding what she'd been through.

Before last night, he'd thought she was a very cool woman, attractive, interesting, someone he'd like to pursue if they weren't in such different social classes. He'd mainly hesitated because he'd felt inadequate: he struggled financially, while she was wealthy.

Last night, learning that her background was far from privileged had changed his view of her. She'd had hard times, grown up rough, lived through experiences most people never dreamed of. She'd seen the worst of people, of men, and yet she'd become a radiant and positive person. He admired that, admired *her*.

Besides that, he couldn't get the look and feel of her out of his mind. The way she'd laughed in the rain. The way her red hair had clung to her arms. She hadn't acted upset that her hairstyle was ruined; she'd had fun with him, like a kid.

And then she'd kissed him like a woman. Every time he thought about that part, he found it hard to breathe.

If there was any way he could be close to her, any way at all, he wanted to make it happen. She was a special, special person. He couldn't stand to just let her go because of the secret knowledge he unfortunately had.

His fists clenched on the steering wheel as he pulled into his sister's driveway. He took deep breaths as he walked inside and greeted Vanessa and Declan with what he hoped was a normal expression on his face.

Right after dinner, Declan ran off to play a video game. Vanessa's plate was still three-quarters full when she stood to clear the table. Her T-shirt and jeans hung on her. Dark circles pulled at her pretty eyes.

"We need to get you into treatment," he said as he picked up the serving dishes and followed her into the kitchen. "You barely ate anything."

She frowned and opened her mouth as if to contradict him, then sighed as she scraped her mostly full plate into the trash. "You're right. I cook stuff, but I can't make myself eat much."

Luke had talked to her about this before, but he still didn't get it. "Don't you get hungry? Like, for a good burger?"

Her forehead wrinkled. "I made friends with hunger, back when I was heavy."

"You were never really heavy."

"Yes, I was. As a teenager." When he didn't agree with her, she went on. "I wasn't obese, but men only started chasing after me when I got really skinny. And I wanted them to chase after me."

Luke closed his eyes for a moment. He'd never been that type of man, but he'd known some.

"It's our culture, Luke. Women who are thin get better jobs, they get the boyfriends, people treat them better…"

He held up a hand. "I'm not sure that's true anymore. But

even if it is, being too thin hurts your health. You passed out! You need to be a healthy weight so you can take care of Declan."

She leaned her back against the counter and nodded. "You're right. I mean, for what it's worth, the way I feel now isn't the same as when I was younger. I'm not so desperate. I'm more just tired, too tired to eat."

"But if you don't eat, you won't have any energy."

"True." She looked out the window, unseeingly. "Maybe it's a control thing. Feels like nothing in my life is controllable except food."

Luke wanted to urge her to seize control, to eat enough to get some energy and then go out and find a job. But he didn't. She hadn't asked for his advice, and she was an adult. "What are you going to do?" he asked her.

"I know I need treatment, like that residential program you showed me. I'll go as soon as I have the money, but since losing my job with Mrs. Ralston-Jones…and I really don't have the energy right now to work for one of the maid companies…well. You already know I'm struggling, because you help with my bills."

"And I'm glad to help you. I want to send you to that program, and I'm working on it." His determination to help his sister got stronger.

She started washing dishes and handing them to him to dry, and for a few minutes they worked in silence, just a brother and sister doing a household chore together. It soothed Luke somehow, made him feel like things were okay and like Vanessa would be okay.

"So, what's bothering *you*?" she asked suddenly.

Busted. "What do you mean?"

She gave him a side-eye glare. "Don't try to kid me. I

know you too well. You've been super quiet, and you didn't pay attention to Declan's stories. So what's going on?"

He drew in a breath and dried another plate. "I'm falling for her."

"For Angie?"

"Yeah." He looked over at Vanessa, trying to read her reaction.

She bit her lip.

"But I don't want to hurt her with what you told me. I'm trying to figure out if it can maybe work between us. Your relationship with her husband wasn't that serious, was it?"

Her head drooped, and she stared into the soapy dishwater, swirling it around with one hand, absently. "In some ways—in one way—it was pretty serious."

His heart sank. "What do you mean? How long did it go on? More than a couple of months?"

She swallowed hard. "It was actually…years."

"What?" He couldn't believe that. He'd been gone for some of Vanessa's adult life, but not that much of it. "How did I not know?"

"It wasn't years of us being romantically involved, but…" She heaved out a breath, let the water out of the sink, dried her hands.

The sound of the water glugging down the drain seemed extra loud. "Just tell me, Vanessa."

"Okay." She sucked in a breath and met his eyes. "Oscar is…was… Declan's father."

Luke stared at her as a sudden coldness hit him at the core. Everything he'd thought about his sister and his nephew shifted and wavered in front of him.

Vanessa looked at him steadily, not speaking. She definitely wasn't joking. Wasn't making this up.

"Oscar…you and Oscar had a… Declan is his *son*?"

She nodded. Her eyes were enormous in her thin face. "But how…"

"Unplanned. Of course." She washed the last glass and handed it to him to dry. "We'd already stopped seeing each other much when I found out. He made me do a DNA test, but once he knew, he was happy about it. Kind of. Gave us gifts, came around to see Declan."

Adrenaline tingled through Luke's body. "Why didn't you tell me? Why didn't you tell *anyone*? Did he pay child support? The man was rich!"

She put a finger to her lips and pointed toward Declan's bedroom. "We can talk more about it, but not when Declan's likely to come in at any second. He knew his dad, but not well. I'm trying to let him know the details a little at a time, when he's ready."

"Of course." Through his confusion and disorientation, he knew his nephew had to be protected. And sure enough, Declan did come in a few minutes later.

Feeling like he had a rock in his gut, Luke hugged them both and left.

As soon as he was off their street, he pulled over in an empty parking lot and sat with his head in his hands.

Angie's late husband was Declan's father. And she had no idea.

The contrast of Oscar's self-assured, entitled personality and Angie's sweet one made him pound his fist on the steering wheel. For that matter, the contrast between Oscar and Vanessa was infuriating too.

Vanessa wore thrift-shop clothes. She and Declan lived in a not-so-great neighborhood, and she sometimes had trouble keeping food on the table. So where was Declan's wealthy father in all of this?

The man's actions had terrible ramifications that were still playing out.

What was Luke supposed to do?

Should he reveal the truth to Angie? She deserved to know it, didn't she? Except the truth would destroy her illusions about her husband. It would crush her.

And yet if he knew the truth and concealed it, then a relationship with Angie wasn't an option. Maybe, if Vanessa and Oscar had had a brief, passing fling, he could have justified keeping the truth to himself. But the fact that Oscar was Declan's father…that was too huge to keep from her. He couldn't do it and be involved with her; it just wouldn't be right. Moreover, it would come out eventually. Declan would grow up and would have to be told the truth. Once he knew, it was just a matter of time until others, including Angie, found out.

After last night, he knew he wanted to pursue this connection with Angie. But now, with what he'd learned…

He let his head rest on the steering wheel. Closed his eyes and prayed: *God, show me the right thing to do.*

A text pinged on his phone and he looked at it. Vanessa.

Please, keep what I told you to yourself. I have a small income from Oscar that stops if the truth comes out.

Luke stared at the words on his phone screen, his breath coming fast, his head spinning.

He sucked in a deep breath, let it out and made his decision.

He couldn't harm Declan and Vanessa by jeopardizing their income. Keeping this ugly reality away from Angie was better for her, anyway. The truth would cause her so much pain.

Which meant he couldn't tell Angie.

And that meant he couldn't be in a relationship with her. Rather than getting closer, as he wanted to do, he had to stop this *thing* developing between them, immediately and completely.

His heart ached as he put his truck into gear and drove toward the carriage house, toward the woman he wanted and could never, ever have.

Angie hummed as she drove home from her morning therapy-dog visits. A whole day had passed since she'd kissed Luke, and she couldn't stop thinking about it.

She'd seen Luke in passing a couple of times yesterday. They hadn't talked, but his smile had been warm, the look in his eyes knowing. They had a secret, together, and it was lovely.

She'd truly never known she could feel so much. She couldn't believe that such a big, powerful man could be so tender and gentle. Moreover, he'd listened with kindness and respect to her history, and he'd still wanted to kiss her.

Maybe she'd been wrong in thinking he was too good and upright of a Christian to have a relationship with her. Maybe being open to others was what being a good Christian was all about.

Maybe, just maybe, this *something* that had started between them would build. Maybe it would grow into something wonderful.

She made a quick lunch, changed into old jeans and a pink T-shirt and checked on Peppy, who'd fallen into her usual post-therapy exhausted sleep. Cavalier King Charles spaniels could be energetic, but they were also perfectly capable of being couch potatoes. That was Peppy after a visit.

Peppy might be tired, but Angie was full of energy. She'd

waited as long as she could, but now, she *had* to see Luke, to talk to him if possible. She practically ran out the back door toward the sound of hammering, only slowing when she neared the last section of fence to be built. This project was closer to done than she'd even realized.

Her steps slowed as she reached the work area. Luke wasn't there. Instead, two men she'd never seen before were fitting together pieces of the kennel.

She approached them hesitantly. "Hi! I'm Angie, the property owner. Where's Luke?"

One of the guys pulled out his earbud, and she repeated the question.

The man gestured toward the far end of the enclosed dog run. There he was, loading up a wheelbarrow. He was sweating, his white T-shirt clinging to his chest. He'd been working hard.

As she watched, he lifted a big cement block and loaded it atop the wood in the wheelbarrow, his strong muscles flexing with the task. Her throat went dry.

This man, this amazing man, had held her in those arms the night before last. She'd told him the worst of her past, and he'd held her. Kissed her.

She walked over, her heart pounding. "Hey, how's it going today?"

He looked up at her, and his eyes darkened. A muscle twitched in his jaw. "Fine."

His voice sounded strange. Flat. Shut down. He lifted the wheelbarrow handles and started steering it toward the main work area.

So he was being businesslike. She tamped down her hurt about that; after all, it was her job he was working on. Maybe he didn't want to lose professionalism in front of the other men.

"I was planning to help you today," she said, trying—and failing—to match his detached tone. "What can I do?"

He paused. Didn't look at her. "It's okay. I brought in some of my contract employees today."

She frowned. "I can't pay over the price we agreed on. Are you sure—"

"It'll get done faster this way, that's all," he interrupted. He started toward the worksite again.

She walked alongside him, struggling to keep up with his pace. Funny, they'd been so in step with each other on Sunday afternoon.

Why did he want to get the job done faster?

"So you don't need me?"

He looked over and met her eyes, and again, that darkness flared in his. "No."

"Well then…okay." She'd wanted to invite him to dinner tonight, but he didn't seem receptive. Slowly, she turned and walked back toward her house.

As she processed his reaction, her steps speeded up and her face heated. She'd rushed out there like she was his girlfriend, but she obviously wasn't. She'd thought the kiss meant something, but it seemed that it didn't.

Not to him, anyway.

A couple of jays chattered at her bird feeder, causing the smaller birds to fly away. Her roses, red and yellow against the white of her house, looked pretty. There was a slight breeze and no humidity, a perfect June day.

She could see that objectively, but she couldn't enjoy it, even when she made herself bend down toward the roses and inhale their fragrance. Sweet, but not as sweet as usual.

Had Luke gone cold because of the things she'd told him about her past?

He'd seemed so understanding, but maybe upon reflection,

he'd decided she was too flawed and fallen for him. She should never have told him the whole truth. Few men could handle that. Luke apparently was with the majority on this one.

Anger arose in her, hot as the sun that beat down on her back. He was a fine one to judge. Like he'd never made a mistake. Like he'd always lived a perfect life. Yes, he'd said he didn't go to men's clubs, and she believed him. But that didn't mean he could stand in judgment over her, did it?

Maybe, to him, it did. A better woman would accept his judgment and stay friendly but distant.

But she couldn't help feeling crushed and disappointed and angry, as if the promise of his kiss had been broken.

She walked into her house and saw the self-help book she'd been reading a few days ago. One of the tenets was that you shouldn't assume you know what others are thinking.

She shouldn't assume he'd passed moral judgment on her and rejected her for what she'd done. That didn't fit with what she knew of the man.

Peppy lifted her head and looked at Angie, then dropped it back to the floor, her eyes closing.

Angie spun and marched out the door. Adrenaline carried her back to the area where Luke and his employees were working. Ignoring the other workers, she approached Luke. "Can I talk to you a minute?"

"Sure." He didn't exactly sound eager, but he did put down his hammer. He wiped his hands and then his brow with a bandanna and followed her to a shady spot beneath the big oak tree.

"Did you cool off toward me because of what I told you about my past?" she demanded.

He looked startled. "No!" He hesitated, then added, "But that kiss was a mistake. We'd do better to keep a little distance."

She waited for an explanation, but none was forthcoming. Two squirrels ran across the yard and up the oak tree, one following the other in what looked like a playful chase. A breeze cooled her warm cheeks.

"So...why should we keep a little distance?" she asked finally.

He looked off to the side, not meeting her eyes. "There are reasons." Again, he didn't elaborate.

Her disappointment tasted more bitter than the worst medicine.

"Okay," she managed finally. She turned and started walking toward the house.

A part of her waited for him to call her name, call her back, explain, pull her into his arms.

But that didn't happen.

She wanted to keep feeling angry and self-righteous, like she was better than him. Instead, she felt like curling up into a ball on the couch and crying.

Chapter Eleven

❧

Wednesday afternoon, Angie got sick of mooning over Luke. Enough already! He'd barely communicated since telling her they needed to keep distance between them. Just a couple of terse texts updating her on the progress of the kennel, which was nearing completion.

Maybe he was afraid she was having a meltdown. Men hated to deal with women's emotions, in her experience. But good news for him: she'd been busy doing therapy visits and speaking to the Rotary Club and the Elks about her project, garnering as much support as she could. In the evenings, rather than allowing herself to brood, she'd researched grants and found several that might work to expand her project. She'd emailed with the administrator of one of them and gotten enough encouragement that she'd started roughing out an application.

She grabbed her car keys and purse and, like she always did when she left the house, told Peppy where she was going. She was just turning away from the dog's soulful eyes when she heard a car door slam outside.

Luke. Just the thought of him being nearby sent her heart into a complicated tailspin. She walked to the kitchen window and looked out.

It wasn't Luke. It was Caleb, emerging from Mrs. Ralston-Jones's old-fashioned Cadillac.

He had to be going to visit Declan, only Declan wasn't here. The spot where Luke always parked his truck was vacant.

Surely the pair couldn't be coming to see her. On the other hand, maybe Mrs. Ralston-Jones had had a change of heart about donating to her cause. She dumped her things on the kitchen counter and walked out.

Caleb rushed to her. "We're going to the shelter today, right?"

"Uh…" In her overly emotional state, she'd forgotten her offer to let Declan and Caleb come to the animal shelter with her.

Mrs. Ralston-Jones lowered her window. "I certainly hope he got this right," she said, "because I have errands to do."

"Sure, I guess." Would Declan still come? Who could say?

"Behave yourself," Mrs. Ralston-Jones said to Caleb. "And remember, you can't get a dog." She accelerated, and the car purred off.

"Where's Declan?" he asked.

"Where's Declan?" she asked at the same time.

"Jinx!" he shouted.

She had to laugh. Kids were the ultimate cure to a bad mood. "Happy last day of school," she said to him.

He rolled his eyes. "I'm so glad it's over."

She remembered him saying he had to do summer school. But now wasn't the time to burst his "school's out" bubble. "I guess Declan will be here soon. He was in class today, wasn't he?"

"Yeah. His uncle picked him up. Can I play with Peppy until they get here?"

"Sure. I'll bring her out."

She watched Caleb running around with Peppy, and long-ing squeezed at her heart. What she wouldn't give to have a child of her own.

Men were a bad risk, at least for her, at least for now. Just look what had happened with Luke. But a child…maybe she could pursue adoption.

Then again, with her background, would anyone even consider letting her adopt a child?

Discouragement nipped at her, but some new energy in-side her pushed it away. If she could get through her bad early years, survive the loss of her husband and raise money to start a new venture that helped people, then she was more than just a former exotic dancer.

She wasn't going to give up without even trying. She was going to look into it. She'd do that much for herself.

Luke's truck pulled in, and immediately Declan jumped out and came running over to Caleb. Luke followed behind, more slowly.

She looked at him and raised an eyebrow but didn't say anything. She wasn't going to bend over backward for him, no sir, not anymore.

He stood a good ten feet away. "I understand you told Declan and Caleb they could come with you to the animal shelter after school today."

"That's right," she said, crossing her arms.

"I hate to say no on their last day of school, but…" He trailed off.

But what? Was he afraid to contaminate them, or him-self, by getting in a car with her? "I'll take them there and bring them back," she said. "When we get home, I'll send Declan back to your place and watch him from my deck until he's safely inside. You and I won't even have to interact." Snarky, but so be it.

"Angie…it's not… I don't…"

She waited, but he didn't seem to have anything more to say. Just a helpless expression on his face.

"I'll go with you," he said finally.

She squashed down the part of herself that was happy he'd offered. They'd had such a good time on their outings before.

He wants to keep his distance, she reminded herself. *He said kissing me was a mistake.*

"No need for that." She'd enjoyed their trips before, but things had changed between them. The last thing she wanted was an awkward car ride with Luke.

"Well, there might be a need." He waved a hand toward Declan and Caleb, who ran madly around, whooping "School's out! School's out!" Even Peppy slunk away from them.

She crossed her arms, waiting.

"They're just too wild," Luke said. "I can't make you manage that. I'm going to come."

"If you want," she said, shrugging.

This wasn't going to be fun.

Luke regretted his decision to ride along to the animal shelter for the entire thirty-minute trip. He and Angie didn't speak a word to one another. Fortunately, the boys were too excited to notice. They chattered and joked and yelled the whole way.

He hated that he'd hurt her. When she'd walked toward him yesterday, smiling that smile, so cute in her ripped jeans and girly T-shirt, he'd barely been able to stop himself from holding her.

The worst part had been watching her expression change from happy and excited to closed and guarded and hurt. He'd done that. He should never have kissed her. With his lack of restraint, he'd raised her hopes that they could be together. Raised his own hopes, too.

Now, her hurt seemed to have morphed into anger.

And that was good, wasn't it? Because now that Vanessa had revealed the truth about Declan's father, Luke was even more certain he could never put his feelings for Angie into action.

If she and Luke got together, she'd end up spending lots of time with her husband's love child. No woman would tolerate that. And if she blew up about it, had a meltdown, told people—which would be a very natural reaction—that would be a disaster, too, for Declan and Vanessa. Relationships in a small town were easily damaged, and gossip ran rampant.

The impossibility of the situation seemed to ride along in the front seat, a silent barrier between them.

What surprised him was how much it hurt. He hadn't realized how much he'd enjoyed his time with Angie, how wonderful their closeness had been, until it had become necessary to push her away. Even before they'd kissed, they'd been on the same wavelength. He'd never connected with a woman the way he'd connected with Angie.

They could have been so good together.

They arrived at the squat, cinderblock building surrounded by a gravel parking lot and a chain-link-fenced area, an outdoor play space for the dogs. Barking echoed through the air as the boys rushed out of the car and headed for the shelter's front door.

"Declan! Caleb!" Luke used his drill sergeant voice, and the two boys instantly turned around. "Come back here. Now."

They stood in front of him, wide-eyed.

"You have to be quiet and respectful in the shelter," he said.

"We will! We will!" they assured him.

Luke didn't believe it for a minute. He turned to Angie, who was waiting, arms crossed. "Maybe you should go ahead and talk to the staff about what you're looking for, get some of the preliminaries done," Luke said to Angie. "I'm going to have the boys do a few laps and push-ups and then see if they're really ready to behave in there."

She nodded and headed inside, and Luke watched her go with a heart full of pain.

Why, oh why had Vanessa made the mistake of getting involved with a married man? Why had that particular married man turned away from his sweet, gorgeous bride and gotten involved with another woman?

And how painful would it be for Angie to learn the truth?

He couldn't pretend that a relationship with him was worth destroying her image of her late husband. No. Better to just keep his distance. Maybe someday they could at least be friends.

There was another reason not to let Angie in on Declan's paternity. Apparently, Oscar had stayed somewhat involved with Declan, his only child, visiting occasionally and sending expensive gifts. That explained how Declan had a couple of toys and video games that neither he nor Vanessa could have ever afforded. It also explained the offhand remarks he'd heard Declan make, sometimes, about "my dad."

Vanessa had told him about the financial arrangement Oscar had made for the boy. It was all a little hazy to Luke, but apparently Oscar had left money for the executor of his will to dole out to Vanessa on a monthly basis…provided that she kept Declan's paternity out of the public eye. It was enough to pay the mortgage on their house, which assured that they'd have a place to live, however humble. He'd also left a trust for the boy's college education, but with the same provision.

Vanessa couldn't reveal the truth because if the executor found out she had, it would cut off the financial support. Not that it was much—to Luke, the amount seemed absurdly low for a rich man—but it explained how Vanessa could get by without working, as long as she was extremely frugal and Luke contributed.

So, he couldn't reveal the truth about Oscar and Vanessa and Declan. That was that.

He was well and truly stuck.

Declan and Caleb ran toward him, panting. "We did… three…laps," Declan said. "Do we hafta do push-ups?"

"Just ten," Luke decided. He pulled a couple of worse-for-wear granola bars out of the side pocket of his work pants and, once the push-ups and complaining about them were done, handed them to the boys. "Remember," he said as they scarfed down the food, "quiet and calm is best for the dogs."

"We'll be quiet!" Caleb shouted at the top of his lungs.

Luke rolled his eyes and followed them into the shelter.

Inside, he spotted Angie walking down one aisle of the shelter, talking with a woman who looked to be an employee, but not Louwana, whom they'd met last time. Angie paused by a pen and knelt down, apparently interacting with the dog inside.

She was so kind and beautiful and good. He didn't deserve a woman like her, even if he could have legitimately tried to date her. He led the boys to the other aisle. The air smelled of disinfectant and a mixture of dog-related odors, and there was a lot of barking, some deep, some high-pitched.

As they walked down the aisle, several of the dogs leapt with excitement to see the three of them. Others cowered at the back of their pens. The boys laughed and shouted, "Look at this one" and "This one's cool!"

Luke put a firm hand on each boy's shoulder. "Quiet and calm," he reminded them.

"Look, Uncle Luke!" Declan knelt by a crate in the corner. Inside was a small, disheveled-looking white dog, yapping at the top of its lungs.

Caleb knelt beside Declan and ran his finger along the dog's name on a white tag. "R…am…bo," he read. It came out like "Rahm-boo."

"I think it's Rambo," Declan said, pronouncing the word correctly over the din.

Funny name for a little white dog. But then again, the creature looked feisty. Maybe he was a "Rambo" at heart.

Declan put his hand flat against the front of the crate. Luke was about to warn him to be careful when the dog stopped barking and started licking Declan through the bars.

"Cool!" Caleb put his fingers through the wires, and the dog licked his hand, too.

No doubt the boys' fingers were full of interesting tastes and smells, since Luke had neglected to have them wash their hands before they'd eaten their snack. Oh well.

Angie and the shelter worker came around the corner. Sunshine from a high window turned Angie's hair golden bronze.

"Look, Miss Angie, we like *this* one," Caleb said. He beckoned her toward the crate where Rambo panted and yipped.

"Yeah!" Declan agreed. "You should get Rambo!"

Angie introduced the boys to the shelter worker, whose name was Virginia. After a little pause, she introduced Luke as well, without once looking at him.

"You should get Rambo for a reading dog," Caleb said. "I'd read to him."

If the dog would settle down and stop yapping. Luke

wasn't sure why the boys had fallen in love with this little creature—it seemed random to him—but Angie responded to their enthusiasm with a smile and a skillful deflection. "I think we have a candidate over on the other side," she said. "Would you like to meet her?"

"Okay!" Declan said, and he and Caleb jumped to their feet.

To the shelter worker, Virginia, Angie explained, "It's good to see how a prospective therapy dog responds to kids, especially since I primarily train the dogs to read with kids."

She continued to ignore Luke.

"Of course. This way, boys." The worker led the way to a pen along the far wall, Declan and Caleb trotting behind her. Angie followed the boys, and it would have been normal for her to chat with Luke, who was a few feet behind her.

She didn't.

You told her you wanted distance. And now you've got it.

After traversing half the row, filled with a mix of large and small dogs, they reached a pen and stopped in front of it. A black German shepherd mix sat alert, tongue out, panting.

"She's big!" Caleb said.

"Is she nice?" Declan asked. "What's her name?"

Angie smiled. "She *is* big, and she's nice. Her name is Coco." She turned to the shelter worker. "Would we be able to use one of the meet-and-greet rooms to see how she does with the boys?"

"Sure thing." Virginia put a harness over the shepherd's head and led the way to a small room that held chairs and a box of dog toys. She led Coco into the room and then closed the half door behind her, allowing the rest of them to watch from outside. She put the dog inside and said, "Sit!"

The dog sat, tail wagging.

Virginia tossed a hot-dog toy, which Coco caught easily. She approached the dog and held out a hand. "Give," she said.

The dog dropped the toy into her hand.

"Wow, cool!" Declan shouted from where he stood beside Caleb, peeking over the half door. "She's smart!"

"Remember, quiet and calm, buddy," Luke said.

Angie took a half step away from him and glanced over without meeting his eyes. "It's fine if they're loud. If Coco is going to work with kids, she needs to be able to handle noise."

"Fine." He stepped back, palms out. Obviously, no input from him was going to be accepted.

"Come on in, boys," the worker said. Soon, Caleb and Declan were tossing toys for the dog to fetch, petting her and basically getting in her face.

The dog handled all of it well, and Virginia stepped out of the room. "You can see Coco is very smart and trainable," she said. "Good temperament, too. I thought of her the moment you told me what you need."

"Wonder why she's available," Luke said.

"Her owner got sick. He's older and facing a lot of medical treatments. Very sad." Virginia frowned. "Add to that, she's all black and she's a shepherd. A lot of people associate that look with police dogs, so they're afraid of her."

Angie nodded, looking thoughtful. "That could be an issue for therapy work, too. I wonder if people will be too scared of her?"

"Maybe," the worker said. "But you could also be a part of the solution. Show people that a dog like Coco can be friendly and sweet."

"Good point," Angie said. "Can I think about it?"

"Sure. We can hold her for a couple of days. But not more

than that. We try to get all our dogs adopted as quickly as possible."

As if to prove her point, a family came into the shelter and approached the reception desk. "Yoo-hoo," the father said. "We're looking for a dog."

Luke already didn't want Coco to go to anyone but Angie. She would put the dog's training to such good use.

After Coco was back in her crate—her alert eyes following them and a tiny whine coming from her throat—Angie turned toward the exit.

Caleb tugged her arm. "What about Rambo?"

"Rambo?"

"That little white dog they were looking at," Luke clarified. Oops. He'd spoken to Angie again. Not allowed, apparently.

Virginia paused and shook her head. "Rambo," she said with a sigh.

"What's his story?" Luke asked. For some reason, the little mop of a dog intrigued him, too.

"If you have time, come along and I'll tell you."

"Sure," Angie said, and they all walked toward the little white dog's crate.

"Rambo was here with his brother," Virginia explained as they walked. "That dog was calmer and, honestly, much cuter. Tiny, with symmetrical gray patches instead of…" She broke off, and Luke filled in the space mentally with almost the same words Declan said: "Black *splotches*."

"Exactly." Virginia smiled at the boy. "Anyway, that dog got adopted out. But Rambo is just so…ornery."

As if to prove her words true, the little dog started barking and jumping at the door of the crate as they approached.

"Mom says *I'm* ornery." Caleb sank to his knees in front of Rambo's crate. Declan did the same.

"And he's older," the worker continued, speaking over the sound of Rambo's yaps. "Eight, we think. He may require some medication for his heart. He's house-trained, but not much else. Probably not what you're looking for."

"Miss Angie, just come look at him." Declan moved aside to make room for Angie at the front of the kennel.

She smiled and sat down cross-legged between the two boys. She was so kind, going along with them instead of getting irritated. Luke hadn't thought it was possible, but his heart melted a little more.

The dog danced with what looked like excitement, still barking. When Angie poked a finger through the wire of the crate, he settled down and licked it.

"Watch this," Caleb said. He put his hand flat against the wire, and again, the dog licked his hand.

The worker slid a plastic baby gate across the aisle, making an enclosure, and then opened the pen. Rambo rushed out and ran around in circles, leaping at the boys and at Angie. When the little dog licked her face, she laughed and grimaced at the same time. "Bad breath, buddy."

Rambo climbed all the way into Angie's lap, turned a couple of times and settled there, panting.

"He sure seems to like you," the worker said. "We'd be thrilled to place him. He does get along well with other dogs, so being around Coco and your dog shouldn't be a problem."

Angie stroked Rambo, who looked up at her with apparent adoration, periodically licking her hand.

The boys sat in front of the pair, watching, the pleading expressions on both their faces oddly similar to Rambo's.

Angie looked at Rambo, then the boys, then at Rambo again. "It's very doubtful," she said, "but I'll think about it."

"Yes!" The two boys high-fived each other.

"Not so fast." Angie held up a hand. "Don't get attached. He needs to find the right home, and it's probably not with me."

"Then with *me*!" Caleb yelled.

Angie shook her head. "I don't think so. Remember what your grandma said."

Still on the floor, Declan tugged Luke's pants leg. "We could take him."

Luke shook his head. "We can't. Your mom and I are both in transition. I work all the time, and it would be too much for your mom right now."

"You know what," the shelter worker said. "Maybe you could foster him for a few days and see. If it doesn't work out, he'll have at least gotten some time in a home. We'll know more about how he does in a home environment. That might help him get adopted."

"It's a good thought." Angie frowned. "I'm going to think about it overnight and get back to you tomorrow about both dogs."

Luke felt useless. Angie could absolutely have handled the boys alone. He didn't need to be here. But at the same time, he loved seeing Angie in action. She was good with dogs and with the boys, not giving in to impulses but open to the unexpected, like Rambo. That was the kind of thing you discovered after dating a person for months. Subtle things that made all the difference.

He'd already discovered them in Angie, and he liked what he saw. A lot. If things were different…

But they weren't. In fact, things kept getting worse. This kid she was now talking to with animation as they drove home was her husband's illegitimate child. And Luke couldn't let her find out.

Not only that, but Declan was getting attached to Angie,

too. He seemed to assume that Luke would live in the carriage house for the foreseeable future.

That wasn't likely. His work for Angie might last another few weeks; before this awkwardness had started, they'd discussed some more detailed improvements to the carriage house, and Luke had tentatively agreed to take them on for more free rent.

Now, he feared she was going to kick him out any minute. If she did, not just Luke, but Declan and even Caleb would be affected by it.

He needed to listen to his own advice and keep his distance from her.

Chapter Twelve

It took a little over a week for Angie to actually get Coco because the dog had developed a case of kennel cough that she needed time to recover from. Finally, yesterday, she'd brought her home. Now, Angie sat on the porch with Coco, stroking the big dog, frustrated. She'd behaved so perfectly at the shelter, obeying all of Virginia's commands. Now, she wasn't willing to sit or give paw, two minor bits of obedience that any neighborhood dog could manage.

To make it worse, Peppy didn't like Coco. She'd cringed when the big dog came near her, her whole body shaking as if Coco meant to hurt her. When Coco had tried to sniff her, she'd bared her teeth, something Peppy never, ever did.

Angie sat back in her deck chair, looking out across the backyard, trying to settle her own emotions. But even the green leaves against a fading blue sky, the sound of birds chirping and singing, the fragrance of climbing jasmine didn't make her feel calm.

Maybe she'd transmitted her own stress to her dogs.

She kept thinking about Luke. She knew she'd been rude to him, or if not rude, then at least cold. But what could he expect when he'd basically rejected her? Not that they'd really had a relationship, just a friendship and one very wonderful kiss. Still, she hurt like a woman scorned, and she'd reacted accordingly.

When she forced her thoughts away from the handsome handyman, they turned to Rambo, the frumpy little dog whom she'd decided to leave at the shelter. She'd realized quickly that it wouldn't work and had told Caleb and Declan.

They'd been upset, begging and cajoling and making logical arguments while she weeded her flower gardens, until Luke came over and stopped them. Later, she'd heard them brainstorming about how to talk their mothers into letting them get the dog. They'd also argued about who would get Rambo first, if both mothers said yes.

Angie was pretty sure that they'd both say no.

So Rambo would stay at the shelter. Virginia, the shelter employee, had completely understood when Angie had let her know, so why did she keep thinking about the feisty little guy?

She needed to focus on her therapy-dog program, not on a completely unsuitable dog. Not on a completely exasperating man.

She went back inside and found some turkey lunch meat. Maybe Coco would respond better to the high value treat. Indeed, when she emerged, Coco caught wind of the turkey and sat up, eyes alert.

"Hey!" Declan and Caleb came out of the carriage house— she hadn't even known they were there—and ran toward Angie and Coco, distracting the dog and disrupting Angie's training plan. Great. She handed Coco a piece of turkey anyway and turned to greet the boys, who really were cute and good kids.

They stopped still, looking from Coco to Angie. "You didn't get Rambo," Declan said, sounding glum.

"She said she wasn't gonna." Caleb reached out a hand for Coco then backed away. "Is Coco gonna bite me?"

"No." That much, she was sure of, or she'd never have brought Coco home.

"How come you didn't get Rambo when you got Coco?" Declan whined.

"I can't get a dog who won't work in a therapy program!" Hearing the sharp sound of her own voice, she forced her face into a smile. "I'm having enough trouble with Coco," she explained. "She doesn't want to focus." Holding out a piece of turkey so Coco could see it, Angie ordered Coco to sit. Slowly, the big dog obeyed. "Give paw," she said. But Coco just stared expectantly at the hand in which she held the turkey. She sighed. "Touch," she said, holding out the hand, and of course, Coco was eager to tap her nose against the turkey-scented hand. She gave the dog the treat.

"It's a lot of change for her," she said, as much to herself as to the boys. "I probably shouldn't try to train her on her first day in a new home."

"Rambo could've done it," Caleb said. Which was complete nonsense. Angie could only imagine what the rambunctious senior pup would have done if sprung from his crate and left to run around an actual yard.

Rambo would've liked it, she thought, picturing the wind blowing through the little dog's thick, messy fur. "Did you talk to your moms about possibly getting Rambo?" she asked. Then realized from their glum faces that it was a sore subject.

"My mom said no," Caleb said, sounding discouraged. "She's a lawyer and she's too busy. Even though I *told* her I'd take care of Rambo."

"And my mom said we couldn't afford it," Declan said.

"It makes sense, but I'm sorry to hear it," Angie said. "I have some cookies. Would you like a couple?"

Declan lifted one shoulder in a shrug. "Okay."

"Yeah," Caleb said.

As she went inside to get the snack, Angie wondered whether Luke knew the boys were over here. Was he just dumping them on her?

She took out the cookies and a couple glasses of milk. "Where's your uncle?" she asked Declan.

"He's working on the kennel," the boy said as he stuffed an entire cookie into his mouth. "He's in a bad mood."

"There's gonna be room in the kennel for Rambo," Caleb said hopefully.

"Aw, honey. He's just not right for the therapy-dog program." Angie ran a hand quickly over Caleb's hair, smoothing down his persistent cowlick.

"How do you know?" Declan asked. "You thought Coco would be good as a therapy dog, but she's not."

"She will be. It's just a transitional time for Coco."

"Same for Rambo," Declan argued. "Just because she's bad now, doesn't mean she always will be. My mom says the past is the past."

Insightful words coming from a rising third grader.

She wasn't going to argue with them, so she just handed them more cookies and leaned back in her chair, stroking Coco's fur. It was probably best to build a relationship with the dog first, before getting into serious training.

"There you are." Luke walked across the yard, a frown on his face. He didn't even look at her. "Don't bother Angie," he said to the boys.

It hurt that she was happy to see him, despite his negative attitude.

"Nobody wants us around." Caleb's lower lip stuck out. "My grandma doesn't, and you don't, and *she* probably doesn't, either." He gestured toward Angie.

"It's fine," she said. "You boys can stay." But they were already grabbing the last two cookies and jogging toward a flock of blackbirds that had settled into the grass. They ran at the birds, waving their arms, causing them to flutter up into the air.

"Caleb and Declan aren't your responsibility," Luke growled.

"True, and yet here they are." If he was going to be all grouchy, she could be, too. "There are summer programs for kids, you know."

Something crossed his face, and she immediately felt bad. "They're expensive, though. They're really welcome to hang out with me," she said.

His mouth twisted to one side. "I'll see what I can do to keep them out of your hair," he said and stomped off.

He was hurt by what she'd said. Angie could almost hear the thoughts banging against one another as he headed toward the woods where the kennel was located and where the boys had disappeared. He thought she was pitying him and Declan, too.

In reality, she felt wistful, seeing how close Luke and Declan were. Having a caring adult relative in her childhood would have made all the difference. It would have helped her weather her mother's emotional storms and her stepfather's rages, maybe shown her what she'd only realized much later: that those adult outbursts were mental health issues that had nothing to do with her.

Maybe Luke's emotions had nothing to do with her, either. Maybe he was struggling with things she didn't understand. They didn't know each other all that well.

Unfortunately, she was well aware that her own blue mood had everything to do with him.

* * *

Two days later, on Saturday, Luke was still seething over Angie's implication. She'd acted like he was too poor to take care of his own nephew. And like he was ignorant of the fact that there were summer programs for kids.

Hello, lady, summer programs don't always start the minute school is out. They actually give the kids a few days off. That was the only reason the boys had been running around Angie's property last week. And since Luke had scolded them, they'd steered clear of Angie's house and porch.

Declan would soon start spending part of each day at a community sports program. And Caleb would be starting summer school next week.

So they had run free for a few days. So they'd visited her and her dogs, once. Was that a crime?

He blew out a breath and shook his head at himself. He wasn't really mad at Angie, he was mad at the situation he found himself in. He felt powerless to solve it, powerless to stop hurting her, powerless to do what he wanted to do.

A minor annoyance was that Caleb's grandmother kept dumping Caleb off at Luke's place. Given Mrs. Ralston-Jones's wealth, Luke was pretty sure the family could afford childcare. But here the boy was today, in Luke's backyard again.

Luke didn't really mind having Declan and Caleb around. This spacious neighborhood, with big backyards set against intriguing woods and a creek that held all manner of crawdads and other critters, was a great place for them to run free. And Luke was here weekends and evenings, working on Angie's projects. Making money that would ultimately help his sister and Declan, both.

Still, he'd meant it when he'd said they weren't Angie's

responsibility. Today was a gorgeous, sunny Saturday, and he meant to keep a good eye on them.

He paused in his sawing, watching the boys as they gathered rocks and rope and boards from his scrap pile. At least they'd cheered up since their disappointment about Rambo the other day. They were whispering and giggling about something, glancing his way.

From Angie's house came the sound of barking, and she appeared at the door, letting Peppy out. She didn't look to the right or the left. Definitely trying to ignore him.

The boys started toward her, drawn inexorably toward the cute pup and maybe on some level toward the dog's beautiful, warmhearted, motherly owner.

"Boys," he called. "Caleb. Declan. Come over here and help me."

They stopped in their beeline toward Angie, turned and came a short distance toward Luke. "Do we hafta, Uncle Luke?" Declan asked. "Can't we just play?"

His nephew's plaintive tone brought back a memory. Two of them, in fact. In the foster family he and Vanessa had lived with the longest, almost two years, the mother had made Vanessa do all the dishes for the family. Meanwhile, the dad had taught Luke to operate a push mower and then ordered him to mow the big yard every week.

Now, Luke realized the value of the skills those good-hearted foster parents had taught them. Back then, he'd resented spending hours sweating under a hot summer sun, pushing a lawn mower. He'd felt like a servant.

One glorious summer Saturday, much like today, their foster parents had looked at each other and then told him and Vanessa to go play, that they would take care of the chores. It had seemed like such luxury to both of them.

Thinking of Vanessa's happy face back then, her chubby

cheeks, Luke's throat tightened. He looked at the two young boys in front of him. "Go on, then," he said sternly. "But stay away from Angie and close to me."

He cut the ends of a couple of two-by-fours to a forty-five-degree angle and laid them down on the ground, fitting them together. He nailed them to the sides of the barnlike shed, making a good-sized square enclosure. Place was already wired for electricity and had water that could easily be hooked up. It would also be easy to expand if her business took off.

As he worked, he thought about the situation with Angie. He'd definitely been grumpy with her after their visit to the shelter. And yeah, he'd been responding to *her* attitude, but she'd been responding to the way he'd pushed her away. It was more his fault than hers, and he ought to apologize.

He started to stand and then sank back down again. What would be the purpose, when he couldn't get close to her anyway? Why reopen that door just to slam it shut again?

He used his angle-grinder to cut a hole for a dog door. Like always, working with his hands soothed him. As he continued his work, the sounds of birds and barking dogs and the occasional car going by on the street were background noises.

Sometime later, he heard a shout. It was Declan, and he didn't sound right. At the same time, he heard agitated barking.

He stood quickly and looked around. Where were the boys?

Angie rushed out as another shout rang out, louder and more hysterical than the one before. "Have you seen the boys?" he asked as she approached at a run. Inside, he was berating himself. Why hadn't he kept them closer? Where were they?

There was another series of deep barks.

"That's Coco," Angie said. They both started toward the sound.

Declan burst out of the woods and ran toward them, and relief washed over Luke…until he saw the blood all over Declan's hands. Coco trotted alongside Declan, and when the boy stopped, she stopped, too, and barked loudly.

Luke's heart was in his throat as he and Angie rushed to Declan. "What happened?" he demanded, kneeling in front of his nephew and looking him over.

"It's not me, it's Caleb," Declan said. "He's hurt!"

Chapter Thirteen

Angie rushed toward the part of the wooded area Declan had indicated, her heart pounding, Luke and Declan beside her. They pushed through undergrowth, brambles scratching her bare legs, rocks nearly tripping her. When she saw Caleb sitting up against a tree and conscious, tears wet on his cheeks but not currently crying, relief made her knees weak.

Peppy sat beside him, tail thumping.

"Caleb! Are you okay?" she asked, sinking to her knees in front of him.

Luke knelt beside her. "Where does it hurt, buddy?"

Caleb held his hand protectively against his chest, hunching over it, his other hand on Peppy's back.

"It's his hand!" Declan pointed to the one Caleb was protecting. "He hammered a nail into it!"

Angie's stomach knotted. "Should I call 911?" she asked Luke.

"Maybe, but first, let me check it out." Luke was focused on coaxing Caleb to reveal his injured hand.

Inspiration flashed. "I'll see if Elizabeth is home," Angie said. "She's an RN."

"Good idea."

Fortunately, the woman was home and answered Angie's call right away.

"Can you come out to the woods behind our houses and bring some first aid supplies? We have a kiddo who may have put a nail through his hand." Angie described the location.

"Be right there," Elizabeth said.

"Thanks." Luke gave Angie a thumbs-up and then went back to examining Caleb's wound. "Looks like this hurts pretty bad," he said to Caleb. His voice was calm and reassuring. It gave Angie the feeling that nothing too bad could happen with Luke around.

It seemed to have a similar effect on Caleb. The boy wiped his eyes and nose on the back of his good hand. "Peppy kept me company." He rubbed the dog's ears. "I pretended I was reading to her."

"Good dog," Angie said. She was glad the dogs had been here for the boys, and that they'd been sensitive enough that one stuck with the injured boy while the other went with the messenger. Not only were the two pups not growling at each other, but they'd worked together.

Luke pulled a bandanna from his pocket and gently wiped around the injury. Drops of blood landed on the ground and on Luke's hands. She could see how Declan had gotten so bloody trying to help his friend.

Elizabeth arrived at a jog, a blue first aid kit in one hand and a water bottle in the other. Angie rose so Elizabeth could get close to Caleb.

"Let's clean the wound," Elizabeth said. "You want to move aside?" she said to Luke. "I was an ER nurse for twenty years."

"Glad you're here." He immediately scooted back, giving her access.

Caleb cringed back against Peppy, his expression fearful.

"Let me take a look, honey," Elizabeth said with authority, and to Angie's surprise, Caleb complied.

Elizabeth studied the wound then pulled out clean gauze. "This will only hurt a little," she reassured Caleb. Before he could protest, she poured water over the wound.

"Owwwww!" Caleb yelled.

"Don't hurt him!" Declan scooted closer to Caleb's side.

"Cleaning a wound like this hurts a little," Elizabeth said matter-of-factly, "but not as much as that nail hurt going in." She squirted something from a small bottle onto a square of gauze and gently wiped at the wound.

Angie stood next to Luke, craning to see, her heart rate slowing as she realized that Caleb wasn't in immediate danger. Luke was breathing hard, too. He reached out a hand to Declan, and the boy ran to his side and buried his face in his uncle's shirt. Luke stroked his hair.

Beside Declan, Coco sat quiet and alert.

"Think he needs a visit to the express care place?" Luke asked Elizabeth.

The older woman shook her head. "No. Bleeding is already slowing down. We'll just hold gauze to the wound until it stops completely. That is, if he's up to date on…tetanus."

"That's a *shot*," Declan said, ruining Elizabeth's effort to be subtle.

"I don't want a shot!" Caleb started to cry. "I want my mom!"

Elizabeth interrupted the outburst with a kind but firm directive. "Hold this gauze against your hand. Not too tight and not too loose." She watched him for a minute then nodded. "Do you know where your heart is?"

Caleb nodded tearfully.

"We want to keep your hand up above your heart if we can," Elizabeth said, and showed him how to prop his hand on his shoulder.

"We'll call your mom. Do you know her number?" Angie

pulled out her phone. "And maybe your grandma? Was she going to pick you up?"

Caleb nodded and rattled off his mother's number. Angie got through right away, and although she tried to sound calm and reassuring, the way Luke had, Megan still panicked. "I'll be right there," she said. "Thank you for helping him."

When she reached Mrs. Ralston-Jones, the woman started scolding immediately over the phone. Angie and Luke should have watched the boys better. They shouldn't have let them play where there were nails lying around.

Angie restrained herself from pointing out that Caleb wasn't really her responsibility, nor Luke's. It had happened on her property, so she shared in the blame. "He's going to be fine," she assured Caleb's grandmother. "We have a nurse here."

When the woman didn't stop her harangue, Angie said, "We've called his mother, too. Just wanted to let you know. I have to go." She ended the call, cutting off the older woman's rant.

Luke was on his phone, too. "Calling his mom," he mouthed, nodding at Declan.

Now that things were under control, Angie felt her tense muscles relax. She smiled reassuringly at Caleb. "You're going to be fine. But what on earth were you doing out here with nails?"

Caleb and Declan glanced at each other, some wordless communication passing between them. Then Declan shrugged. "We wanted to build our own kennel out here," he said.

"'Cause then we could get Rambo!" Caleb added.

"Declan!" Luke shook his head. "Oh, man."

Guilt pierced Angie. Her therapy-dog program was supposed to help children, not cause injury. And would this even have happened if she hadn't been snarky to Luke about leaving the boys with her?

One glance at Luke told her he felt guilty, too. Finally, he spoke. "Declan, you know if you're upset about a rule or an adult's decision, you need to talk about it, not go off and do your own thing."

"You didn't listen," Declan mumbled.

Angie and Luke both winced, and their gazes met and lingered. Angie wanted nothing more than to pull Luke and Declan into a hug. Handling this emergency had pushed her conflict with Luke out of her mind. Why had she been so mad at him, anyway?

Elizabeth checked Caleb's wound and nodded, her expression satisfied. "Let's get these kiddos back to your house. His bleeding has stopped, but I'd like to see him settled down in a cleaner place than the woods."

Slowly, they walked the boys back to Angie's deck, the dogs walking alongside them, arriving just as vehicles started pulling into the driveway. Megan and Mrs. Ralston-Jones arrived at the same time. Vanessa was close behind.

Megan rushed to Caleb, who burst into tears at the sight of his mom. She sat on the edge of Angie's deck and pulled the boy gently onto her lap.

Peppy flopped down and put her head on her paws, watching the proceedings. After a moment, Coco lay down beside her.

Vanessa gasped when she saw Declan's bloodstained shirt.

"It's not his blood," Luke quickly explained.

"He was trying to help his friend," Angie added, nodding at Caleb.

After hugging Declan tight, Vanessa looked over at Luke. "He's really okay?"

"Declan is fine, just a little shaken up," Luke said. "We're going to have a long talk about safety and making good choices, but now might not be the time."

"I should have been here," Vanessa lamented. "I didn't even get the job I applied for. That interview was a waste. I should have been with my kid."

"Yes, you should have," Mrs. Ralston-Jones said. She stood, arms crossed, surveying the scene. "Why weren't these boys supervised?"

"By whom, Mom?" Megan sounded frustrated. "I thought you were taking care of Caleb."

The older woman threw her hands up in the air. "I can only do so much!"

Angie looked away. It wasn't her business, but it seemed like every time she saw Declan, she saw Caleb as well. It was almost to the point where Luke should be getting child-care pay for Caleb.

Megan was examining Caleb's hand. "I don't think the nail really went through your whole hand, did it?"

Caleb shrugged, but Elizabeth spoke up. "It didn't. Seems like it probably glanced off the side. He might have hit himself with the hammer, too, so there will be bruising. But in my view, he'll be fine. He may not even need to go to the doctor, if you know how to change a dressing."

"I don't want to go to the doctor," Caleb said. "I don't want a shot."

"You're up to date on tetanus shots, so you won't need another one of those," Megan said, her arm still around her son. "See, boys, this is why you get shots when you go to your checkup. It's to keep you safe in emergencies."

Looking relieved, Caleb sidled away from her and put his uninjured hand on Peppy's back. "Peppy kept me company!"

"That's awesome." Megan looked gratefully at Angie. "I'm so glad you all, and the dogs, were here to help Caleb."

"Aren't you going to punish the boy?" Mrs. Ralston-Jones asked. "Both boys, really," she added, frowning at Vanessa.

"The boys' parents can handle the discipline," Luke said firmly.

"I'm not punishing him for getting hurt, Mom!" Megan added.

Angie expected Mrs. Ralston-Jones to argue, but instead, she plopped down on the edge of the deck beside Megan, her face sinking into her hands. "I can't do this," she said, her choked voice carrying to all of them. "That's why I keep sending Caleb off to play with other people, and now look what happened."

Megan sighed and put an arm around her mother. "I've been asking too much of you," she said. "I'm going to have to do some thinking, make some hard choices."

"Are you gonna send me to military school like Gramma said?" Caleb asked.

Declan's eyes widened. "Will I have to go?"

"Nobody's going to military school," Vanessa said, "or at least, Declan isn't."

"Nor is Caleb. I don't know where you got that notion," she added, rolling her eyes at her mother. "I think it's time we go home. Thank you so much for everything you did," she added, hugging Luke, Angie and Elizabeth in turn, and kneeling to give Peppy an ear rub and a kiss on the top of her head. "I owe you all."

"You have a great kiddo," Angie said as she walked Megan and Caleb to her car.

"Thanks. You know, you should go out with me and Gabby sometime. Not that either of us has much free time, but we try to get together for a girls' night every now and then. You'd be welcome."

"That would be great!" Angie was a little surprised at

the invitation, but pleased. She didn't have many girlfriends in town.

After Caleb and his people had driven off, Angie brought out water bottles and a bowl of pretzels.

Luke and Declan instantly drained their water, and Angie laughed and handed them each a second bottle.

Then she turned to Elizabeth. "Thank you so much for helping out. I'm sure you had other things planned for your morning."

"Not a problem. I've bandaged up my grandkids and other neighborhood kids many times." She stood. "This afternoon, I'm doing my baking for Father's Day this weekend. We'll have a full house."

"My dad's dead," Declan volunteered out of nowhere.

Luke and Vanessa exchanged concerned glances. Angie patted Declan's shoulder. "That must be hard for you sometimes," she said.

Declan shrugged. "*He* comes to all my Father's Day stuff," he said, pointing to Luke. "I don't remember my dad that well. He was too busy to visit us very often."

It was all said in a matter-of-fact voice, but it made Angie's heart ache. The young boy's words, along with today's accident, put everything into perspective for Angie. Her disagreements with Luke weren't important, not in the grand scheme of things.

Declan sat on the ground and clicked his tongue to the two dogs. Coco instantly went into a play bow. Peppy flopped down beside Angie, and Declan found a ball and started throwing it for Coco.

"Looks like Coco's becoming part of the family," Elizabeth said. Then, in a tone that was low enough only to be heard by the adults, she added, "I'd like to invite you all to our Father's Day celebration, but we're going to be bursting at the seams."

Vanessa and Luke thanked her and waved off the invitation, assuring her she'd already gone above and beyond by helping Caleb.

Angie saw a way to make up for what had happened here today. "If you're free," she said to Luke and Vanessa, "I'd love to have you over for a Father's Day lunch after church."

Then she wondered why the pair of them looked so odd as they accepted the invitation.

On Father's Day, Luke wasn't surprised that the breakfast Declan and Vanessa had prepared for him sat heavy in his stomach.

For one thing, Declan had way overdone the hot sauce on the eggs. For another, Vanessa had only pretended to eat her breakfast, hiding her eggs under her toast and hastening to clean up, which meant that she'd thrown her food away. Not because she didn't like it, but because she was drifting further into her disordered eating.

No wonder; they were both incredibly nervous about the lunch visit to Angie's later that day.

When Declan went upstairs to shower and dress for church, they talked about it. "Maybe we should just cancel," Luke said. "I know you like Angie, and Declan obviously does, but given the issues…"

"I know." Vanessa stirred half a teaspoon of sugar into her black coffee. "It's scary. I *do* like Angie. I'd even like to be friends with her, if things were different. If we cancel, though…" She trailed off.

"Right. If we cancel, it'll hurt her feelings, but…" He sighed. "That's nothing I haven't done before. We can cancel."

Vanessa frowned. "No, Luke. I've caused you so many problems, taken so much from you—"

"Stop." He put a hand on her arm. "You're my sister and I love you, and I always want to be here for you. That's my first priority."

She shook her head. "It *shouldn't* be. *I* shouldn't be. You're a great uncle to Declan, but you should have the opportunity to build a family and become a father to your own kids."

He shrugged. "Someday. Maybe."

His sister held up a hand. "Don't be dense, Luke. I can tell you like Angie a lot. You and she would be good together. Don't you want to see if it can work?"

"Sure, I'd like that," Luke admitted. "But if she finds out the truth about you and Oscar..."

Vanessa buried her face in her hands, shaking her head back and forth. Then she looked up at him. "I am so, so sorry I made the mistakes I did. Not sorry to have Declan, not ever, but sorry it happened with a married man, however unintentionally on my part."

"We have to let the past go," he said. "We've both made mistakes, but the future can be better. Maybe..." He leaned back in his chair and looked out the window, then back at his sister. "What do you think would happen if we told her the truth?"

Vanessa tilted her head to one side, her forehead wrinkling. "I don't know. I think she'd be pretty upset by it. I know I would be, if the situation were reversed."

His sister was probably right, but maybe...could they both be underestimating Angie? She'd had a lot of bad experiences in her life and had come through them stronger. Maybe she could handle the truth about Declan.

"You know," Vanessa said slowly, "Oscar wasn't that big a part of Declan's life. And he's gone now. Declan even said his dad was dead the other day, so there would be no reason for Angie to open up a conversation about him. Maybe we can just keep the truth kind of…quiet."

"As in, don't tell her." Luke stood and took his coffee cup to the sink. "I don't think dishonesty is a good basis for a relationship, and I know Angie would be upset if she found out I'd hidden such a big thing from her."

Vanessa stood and hugged him. "I just don't want to be the reason you don't find happiness. Let's go this afternoon and think more about what to do. If you feel like you need to tell her, then…you can do that. It would probably take you away from me and Declan because I can't imagine that she'd be comfortable seeing him—and especially seeing me—after finding out the truth. And I can't deny I'm worried about losing the money Oscar set aside for me as long as I keep the truth quiet. But that's a sacrifice I'm willing to make if I have to."

Luke could see the concern in her eyes, behind her brave words. Vanessa wasn't very strong, not right now. To lose her closeness with Luke, plus whatever money Oscar had provided for her, might set her way back. And what of Declan?

"You're not going to lose me, no matter what," he said. "But yes, let's go this afternoon. See how things go. It's possible that Angie would handle it better than either of us thinks."

That afternoon, Luke tossed the last cornhole bag, missed and groaned along with Declan as Angie and Vanessa high-fived each other, celebrating their victory.

"Never underestimate the power of a woman," Angie said, giving Luke a sassy smile.

His heart skipped a beat as he looked at her, green eyes sparkling, red ponytail shining in the sun. She wore white shorts and a green T-shirt that said *It was me, I let the dogs out*. She wore no makeup that he could see, and she was gorgeous. A natural beauty.

He was a goner. He'd been attracted to women before, of course, and he had liked women as people and as friends. Rarely had the two feelings, attraction and friendship, come together.

In Angie, they did.

She'd had difficult times in the past, but they hadn't destroyed her, they'd made her more thoughtful and empathetic. She could understand people like Luke and Vanessa, who hadn't grown up in luxury. She was kind, reaching out to steady Vanessa as she stepped up on the deck, and she didn't seem nosey about why Vanessa would need steadying. Luke could easily picture his sister and Angie as friends.

They plopped down in deck chairs, all except Angie. It was a hot afternoon, and they were all sweating. Luke's shirt was sticking to his chest.

Angie went inside and came out with lemonade and iced tea, and they all drank big glasses. Vanessa had eaten a little more than usual, too. It was obvious that she liked Angie and that the feeling was mutual.

Declan had played some with Brian and Elizabeth's grandkids, and Luke was glad the boy had had a good day. No mention of his dead father, thankfully.

The adults sat quietly, talking and resting, but Declan soon jumped up and started throwing a ball for Coco and Peppy. Peppy lay down in the shade after a couple of throws, but Coco kept running, her tongue out, panting loudly. "That's an energetic dog," Vanessa said. "I couldn't run in this heat, let alone in a black coat."

"I know. I think she'd run until she dropped, but we'd better not let it get to that point." She stood and walked over to Declan and spoke quietly. He looked disappointed for a minute and then nodded and ran into the house, belatedly coming back to the doormat to wipe his feet.

"I told him Coco needs practice listening to someone read," Angie explained. "He's going to get a picture book out of my study and read to Coco."

"Good idea." Luke smiled at Angie. She was so good with dogs *and* kids. And she seemed to be over her irritation with him. They'd been talking in a friendly way all through dinner and cornhole.

Maybe this could work. Maybe he'd find a way to tell Angie the truth, if not now, then after Vanessa had gone through treatment and was better equipped to accept the consequences.

Declan came out of the house, a *Wimpy Kid* book in one hand and a framed photo in the other.

Luke caught a glimpse of the photo. He didn't immediately recognize the older man in the picture, but he did recognize Angie, resplendent in a sequined evening gown. His heart skipped a beat.

Vanessa must have seen the photo, too. She stood quickly, her eyes wide.

Declan didn't notice his mother's reaction, nor Luke's. He went straight to Angie and held out the photo. "Hey, Miss Angie," he said. "How come you have a picture of my dad?"

Chapter Fourteen

Angie took the photo Declan was holding out. It was one of her favorites. She and Oscar had taken a cruise for their fifth anniversary, and someone had snapped a casual photo of the two of them laughing together.

Declan stood in front of her, looking expectant. She smiled at him. "What did you say about your dad, honey?"

Declan pointed at Oscar. "*That's* my dad. How come you have a picture of him and you?"

"That's not your dad," she said. "That's—"

A chair scraped as Luke stood abruptly. He was beside Declan in two giant steps. "Hey, buddy," he said, "Coco really wants you to read to her. Look!"

"But Coco's asleep, Uncle Luke."

Angie looked over at Coco. Sure enough, the dog lay on her side in the cool grass, sleeping.

Angie was totally puzzled now.

She looked at Luke's face, and everything inside her stilled. His eyes, closed midway, were dark with some intense emotion she couldn't read. Something Declan had said…

Vanessa cleared her throat. "Declan, c'mere." Her voice shook.

Declan took the photo from Angie, turned to his mom and

walked over to where she was sitting. "Look, Mom," he said, pointing at the picture. "It's Dad!"

Angie looked from Vanessa to Luke. They both had the expression of deer caught in headlights. "I don't understand."

Declan pulled away from his mother and walked back over to Angie, the photo still in his hand. "That's my dad," he said, holding up the picture and pointing at Oscar. "He's dead now."

Angie's breath came faster and heat rushed to her face. She looked into Declan's sweet, innocent eyes. They were the same color as Oscar's, a rich brown. Declan's hair was golden brown, too, but Oscar's had been…white. Brown before that, in pictures she'd seen.

Oscar didn't want children, though. He'd insisted on that.

Two squirrels ran across the yard, chasing each other. Peppy lifted her head and barked once. Coco stood, took a halfhearted few steps toward the squirrels then lay back down. A breeze ruffled the leaves of the lilac bush next to the porch.

The chair arms felt rough beneath Angie's fingers. That was because she was squeezing them so tightly. She tried to relax her hands. Tried to take a deep breath but couldn't.

"Are you sad?" Declan looked down at the picture. "I am, sometimes. Was he your friend?"

A giant rock seemed to have wedged itself in her throat. She reached for her glass. Knocked it over. She nodded slowly as the man, the marriage, the world she'd thought she understood crashed down around her. "Yes, Declan," she choked out. "He was my friend."

Luke's stomach churned like the bay in a storm. He should know how to handle this. A smart man could find the right thing to say, the right words to fix it all.

He looked from Vanessa's anguished face to Declan's confused one to Angie, whose eyes were hollows of devastation as she stared at Declan.

No clue. He had no clue how to handle this. He'd been raised in families that brushed conflict under the rug or expressed it by throwing chairs and kicking down doors and yelling.

He hurt for everyone here. But while he could easily fix a broken appliance, he couldn't fix this. It really wasn't fixable.

Declan jumped off the deck and ran over to Coco and Peppy. "Good girls," he said in an oddly quiet voice. Then he sat down in between them and stroked their heads, not looking at the adults. Which made sense to Luke. Declan had chosen the most together creatures in this yard to hang with.

Vanessa stood, and automatically Luke moved to her side. But she shook her head, so hard that tears flew off her face, and he felt their wetness on his own. "You stay and help her," she said, gesturing toward Angie. "Declan and I will go home."

He took a step toward Angie.

She turned her face away from him and covered it with her hands, her posture hunched and defensive.

"Declan," Vanessa called, her voice strained and husky. "Come on. We're leaving."

"But I was gonna read to Coco!"

"No. Come on, now." Vanessa walked over to him, took his hand and pulled him to his feet. Then she marched him toward the car, ignoring his protests.

The car started. Its engine was noisy as it drove away.

Then, silence.

Luke walked over to Angie. He took the chair beside her. She turned away. She wasn't making a sound.

Peppy came over and nudged her, and she scooped the dog up, not looking at Luke, not facing him.

"Angie, I'm so sorry you found out this way. I...this must be so hard. What can I do to help? Do you want some water?"

"Oscar was Declan's father." She sucked in air, audibly. Then, Peppy in her arms, she turned toward Luke. "I just have one question," she said. "Did you know?"

"I..."

"You knew," she said. Her voice, normally low and a little raspy, now sounded choked.

"I... I did, Angie. I just found out—"

She stood, clutching Peppy. "Come, Coco," she called, and the black dog loped over. She picked up the picture that had started everything, walked into her house with the dogs and slid the glass door closed.

Luke sat on her deck, slumped with shame. This was all his fault. If he hadn't been so foolish as to get involved with Angie, none of this would have happened.

He walked over to the carriage house, feeling ninety years old and like he was carrying a weight way heavier than the heaviest tool bag he'd ever lifted. Some last gasp of an impulse made him pause briefly, hand on the railing, and whisper "Help, Lord." Then he climbed the stairs into the carriage house and sat down on the couch. He leaned his head back, eyes closed.

After he'd sat there a long time, his emotions churning, the title of a sermon he'd heard recently came to him: *Are You Trying to Carry It Alone?*

He'd been trying to carry it alone. He should have been asking God for help and guidance all along, but he hadn't, not enough. Sure, he prayed every day, and he'd prayed for Angie and Vanessa and Declan. But he'd never really asked for help handling everything involved. He'd thought if he worked hard enough and was all things to all people, he could make things work out.

He'd been mistaken.

He leaned forward, his head in his hands, and with very few words, he asked his heavenly Father to show him how to make it right.

Half an hour later, he rose. Still discouraged, worried and sad, but a little less so. He called his sister.

To his surprise, she answered right away. "Where have you been? I've been trying to call you."

"Phone was off. Do you need me to come get Declan?" This emotional maelstrom could make his sister's sickness come back in full force.

"I'm fine. Declan's fine." Vanessa sounded almost impatient. "You need to deal with Angie. Help her understand."

But how could he do that when he himself didn't understand the situation, not really? Vanessa had explained it in a very minimal way, and those facts had come out today with Declan's innocent questions. He didn't really have anything to add.

"I feel so awful to have hurt your relationship with her," Vanessa said, her voice breaking. "Talk to her, Luke! Tell her what you know and what you feel."

"Maybe. Okay." After urging Vanessa to get in touch if she needed him, anytime day or night, he ended the call and stood, undecided.

He'd prayed for God's guidance. Maybe that was coming through his sister. Could it be that, if he communicated the way Vanessa had urged, Angie would come to understand the situation? The reasons why he hadn't told her what he knew?

Seeing no other options, he strode over to Angie's place and knocked on the front door. When there was no answer, he rang the doorbell. His slight burst of optimism was already dissipating. Of course she wouldn't want to answer. He'd related to her under false pretenses. Why would she want to be friends with, or even speak to, a liar?

And the truth was, he wanted way more than friendship, but it looked like that wasn't to be.

He was about to turn away when the door opened. Not all the way, about six inches.

"Angie! Please, let's talk this through—"

"When is Declan's birthday?"

The question threw him for a minute. "Um, let's see, October 22."

"And he's eight, right?"

"Yes. He'll be nine in—"

But he didn't need to finish his sentence because she backed away. Then the door closed. The lock turned with a click.

Whatever hope he'd had of an easy reconciliation disappeared with that quiet little click.

He wanted to throw himself into the construction dumpster he passed as he trudged back to his place. He felt like the trash that filled it. Worthless.

Angie went into her study and sat on the floor, crosslegged, beside a shelf of photo albums. She'd kept them meticulously throughout the eleven years of her marriage. When she'd married Oscar, she'd looked around to see what the wives of his friends did, their duties, their behaviors. Making photo albums had been part of the job description.

Declan was eight years old. She tried to do the math in her head, but she was so upset and confused that she couldn't. She grabbed her phone and opened the calendar app.

He'd be nine on October 22. She counted back the years and got to the year of his birth.

Tears made it hard to see the small numbers on the calendar. Had Oscar been present at the birth of his son?

Was this all even true, or some horrible nightmare?

She dashed tears from her eyes with the back of her hand and counted backward. Nine months before October was... January? That was when, if all this was true, Declan had been conceived.

Running her fingers along the photo albums, she found the one she wanted and pulled it out.

In mid-January of that year, Oscar had taken Angie on a Caribbean cruise.

Had Oscar been with Vanessa before or after the cruise? How long had they been together, anyway? Had the cruise been a guilt offering?

How had she not known? She'd been such a dupe.

Her breath heaved and her throat ached. She'd thought Oscar loved her.

She flipped through that album and the one before, remembering the parties and the trips and the cultural events. Oscar had been so much more sophisticated than she was, and he'd been the leader in their marriage and their social lives. She had gone along gladly. Never before had she been treated so well nor seen such luxury.

She studied herself in the pictures, trying to remember the woman she'd been back then. It had been early in their marriage. He'd been working a lot, like always.

Only maybe he hadn't been working.

A couple of candid photos showed the two of them together, not smiling. There had been arguments, she remembered now. Primarily, when she was pleading for them to have a baby, and he'd said no, he was too old.

Only, obviously, he wasn't too old.

He'd made a baby with Vanessa. Why wouldn't he make

one with Angie? Why would he force her to live through lonely days and nights, rattling around in the house alone, finding ways to occupy herself because she didn't have the kids she'd dreamed of and longed for in her heart?

She wrapped her arms around her upraised knees, making herself as small as possible, trying to soothe the ache in her chest. Peppy pressed close to her side, and Coco lay nearby, head on paws, watching her.

She wasn't good enough to be told the truth, not by Oscar and not by Luke.

She wasn't good enough to have Oscar's baby.

Plenty of "not good enough" thoughts had raced through her head before, taken up residence there. This time, though, they didn't feel quite right. Was she *really* not good enough? Or rather, was anyone good enough? Not really. That was why Christ had died for all of their sins.

Restless, she sat up. She looked at the photo album where it lay open, at Oscar's distinguished, smiling face. His distinguished, smiling, *lying* face.

She kicked the photo album across the room, hard, making both dogs jump. It crashed into the leg of the desk and lay open, several pages crumpled.

As she stood, she saw the photo that had started this whole wretched day of discovery. She'd reflexively put it back in its place when she'd walked into this room.

Picking it up, she looked at the image. The woman she'd been. The man Oscar had been, versus the man she'd thought he was.

Declan had looked at the photo and seen a father. His father. He'd asked what she, Angie, was doing with his father.

Did that mean Oscar had spent time with Declan? Spent time with Declan and Vanessa, that horrible woman? While Angie had played the patient wife, again per the example of other corporate wives, never complaining, Oscar had been out enjoying his lover and his child.

Drawing her arm back, she threw the picture with all her might. It hit the wall and the glass shattered.

It should shatter. It was a lie.

She lay down on the floor and wept. The two dogs, Coco on one side and Peppy on the other, pressed close against her.

After some stretch of time, she sat up then stood. She grabbed a handful of tissues and wiped her eyes and face. Then she clapped her hands gently for both dogs to follow her out. She shut the door behind her. She'd clean up the results of her temper tantrum tomorrow, before glass could hurt the dogs' tender feet.

"You're my best friends, you know that?" she said as she led them downstairs. Peppy really was attached to her, and Coco was getting that way, and both of them were better, way, way better, than lying, deceptive men.

Luke had known the truth, and he hadn't told her. He'd brought Declan around her, knowing that the child was Oscar's. How could he do such a thing to her?

She grabbed her phone and composed a text.

I'd like you out before the end of the month.

She hesitated, her finger poised over the Send button. She thought about all the other things she could say: That she didn't want Declan around, that they should both stay away. That he was a horrible person, and she was crushed. That she never wanted to see him again.

But she was making that attitude evident by her behavior. Maybe she didn't need to spell out the end of their burgeoning whatever-it-was, the friendship that had ebbed and flowed and grown into more. That kiss.

Still carrying the phone, she reached the kitchen and sat down in a chair, facing away from the carriage house. Still, she wondered where Luke was. Had he gone to Vanessa? Had Declan been told the whole truth? She couldn't wish that on the child. He should be raised to think of his dad as honorable, even though he wasn't.

She'd thought of Oscar as a good man, too. She kept remembering more and more moments in their marriage that now had to be reframed. Gifts of jewelry or clothes, which had made her feel special and loved, might well have been guilt offerings. His excitement in taking her to a new restaurant he'd discovered: well, whom had he discovered it with?

How many of his friends had known he was unfaithful? Pete, for example, now in the assisted-living place she and Luke had visited. He'd made some admiring comment about how Oscar liked the ladies.

At the time, Angie had brushed the remark aside. Not anymore. Pete had known.

And if he knew, how many others did? Did people laugh behind her back about how gullible she was?

Picking up her phone, she reread the text asking Luke to leave. Yes. She had little enough power in this situation, but she did have some.

She hit Send.

Chapter Fifteen

On Wednesday evening, Angie was still alternating between hurt and rage.

She wanted to hammer her fists against Oscar's chest and wail about how unfair it was that he'd hurt her. She'd tried to be a good wife, tried hard to make sure he was happy. And yet he'd turned to someone else. Why, why, why?

Since Oscar wasn't here, she spent a good amount of time internally raging at Luke. He should have told her the truth about Declan right away, instead of letting her come to care for the child. She'd been right to send him that text telling him to be gone by the end of the month.

She *had*.

Maybe he was just trying to be nice, to protect her, a voice inside her said. After all, *he* wasn't the one who'd caused Oscar to cheat. That honor belonged to his sister, and to Oscar himself.

It was a circle she'd gone around and around in the past few days, and things weren't becoming any clearer. Mostly, she just felt numb. How could Oscar have betrayed her like that? And then died, so she couldn't demand an explanation?

Suddenly, something else occurred to her: had Oscar provided for Declan in any way?

He'd spent time during his illness closeted with Josiah,

his lawyer. Supposedly, they'd been discussing dry financial issues that wouldn't interest her. But maybe he'd been setting up some kind of trust. Maybe that was why the estate was taking such a long time to settle.

Had he provided for this son she hadn't known he'd had? But if so, why did Vanessa live so humbly? It just didn't make sense.

Her grief about her husband's death had been clean before. She'd been terribly sad, but she'd also known it was coming. They'd said their goodbyes, said what needed to be said.

Although not all of it, at least from his side.

She picked up the dog-training book she'd been reading and then flung it on the couch. She'd find something to watch on TV. She was flipping channels when there was a knock on her door. A few seconds later, the doorbell rang.

Luke. It had to be Luke. Her heart thumped like the beating of a drum as she marched to the door.

Only it wasn't Luke. It was Megan and Gabby, crowded together under one big umbrella. "Come on," Gabby said. "We're taking you out."

"To a fun restaurant," Megan said. She must have read Angie's look of confusion because she added, "It's kind of an apology for my mom chewing you out last week, when Caleb got into that accident. He's fine, and it was definitely his own fault, but Mom can be pretty mean. So I'm buying you dinner and one of those fruity little drinks with an umbrella in it."

Angie had no idea how to respond to their invitation. She liked the women, but she wasn't exactly in a festive mood. All she could think to say was, "I, uh, I don't drink."

"Neither do we." Gabby flung back her hood. "So, girlfriend, are you in?"

"Why not?" Angie shrugged.

Twenty minutes later, she knew why not. It turned out that Gabby was friends with Vanessa, had become friends with her after having Declan in class. "Vanessa told me you might need cheering up," Gabby said after they'd been seated. The restaurant was hopping around them. They were on a covered patio, and the storm of earlier had blown over, leaving everything washed clean and a fresh view of the bay.

"Vanessa is such a nice person," Gabby enthused.

Angie's jaw clenched. She wanted to scream, "No, she's not, she sleeps with married men! Has children by them!"

She wasn't going to do it, but neither could she sit and listen to a love song to Vanessa. "I'm sorry," she said, "but Vanessa and I, uh, we don't get along. Could we talk about something else?"

Megan looked startled, but Gabby nodded. "She said you'd had a disagreement."

Angie's stomach churned. She pressed her lips together to keep from saying what she was thinking: *A disagreement? You call having an affair with my husband a disagreement?*

"Let's see, change of subject," Megan said tactfully. "How about Caleb's improvement in reading? He's not at grade level, not yet, but he doesn't hate to pick up a book anymore. And that's after just one official and one unofficial session with Peppy. I can't tell you how grateful I am, nor how enthusiastic about this program you're building."

"I'm so glad." In the midst of her emotional turmoil, another feeling came in: satisfaction. She'd done something good for Caleb, for other kids, too. "Reading has made a huge difference in my life. I'm thrilled to see someone else catch the reading bug, too."

"Well, I appreciate that more than you know. Now, tell us about you and Luke." She flashed a grin at Gabby and then at Angie. "You make such a good couple."

"No, we don't." Angie barked out the words and then held out a hand. "Sorry. You guys caught me in a bad mood. I shouldn't have come." She lifted her hot face to the breeze. *Please, Lord, just get me through this dinner and back home.*

"We specialize in healing bad moods," Gabby said. "But I will say, if someone looked at me the way Luke looks at you, I'd definitely give him a chance."

"No, you wouldn't." Angie pushed aside the part of herself that wanted to ask: *How, exactly, does he look at me?* "Do you know what you want to eat?" she asked, hoping to get the meal over with quickly.

"Sure," Gabby said. She waved down their waiter. "We're finally ready to order," she said. Without consulting either Megan or Angie, she asked for two seafood platters to split between them, one fried and one broiled. "They're huge," she explained.

Angie blew out a breath. Gabby was definitely the take-charge type. Probably went with her job as a second-grade teacher, but inviting Angie out to try to convince her to make up with an awful woman like Vanessa was going too far.

They did manage to discuss other things, including Caleb and Mrs. Ralston-Jones. Megan was trying to figure out how to lighten her workload so she wouldn't have to lean so heavily on her mother for Caleb's care. Angie, feeling bad about how she'd snapped at the two women, offered up Peppy as a reading companion whenever Megan needed her. They went on to talk about therapy dogs and service dogs in general, since both women were dog lovers and fascinated by Angie's project.

Their seafood platters arrived then, huge as promised. They dug in, and the food was wonderful enough to distract Angie, at least a little, from her misery.

When they were finishing up, Gabby said, "Look, I don't

know what's going on with you, but I would like to pray for you. Do you want me to pray for something specific?"

Angie blinked. She wasn't used to public prayer, but she definitely needed all the help and support she could get. She drew in a breath and let it out slowly. "For healing the past," she said. "I…had some tough times, and they've left scars."

It felt a little heavy to say that to these women she didn't know well, but she desperately wanted to get past the shame of what she used to do for a living. Somewhere in the past few days, she'd come to the conclusion that her own low self-esteem, amplified by her years of dancing, had made her vulnerable to Oscar's deception and manipulation. She hated to think of Oscar that way, and maybe it hadn't all been conscious, but what he'd done was terribly disrespectful and unloving. She hadn't deserved that.

Megan and Gabby exchanged glances. "Healing the past," Megan said. "That is a brilliant prayer that almost anyone could use. Both of us in particular, but those are stories for another day. We just have to remember that we're new creations in Christ."

Right there at the table, she held out her hands. The three of them prayed together.

Soon afterward, they left the restaurant. Angie didn't feel exactly healed, but the other women's hugs, plus the prayer, seemed to bring a small measure of peace into her heart.

On Thursday, Luke put in an eight-hour day and arrived home at four. A short day in his world, especially this week.

Ever since the blowup at Angie's on Sunday, he'd kept busy with extra handyman work, getting his paying jobs all caught up. He'd come home each night to work on the carriage house late into the evening.

He had to. Angie wanted him out by the end of the month.

He was more than on track to finish work on the carriage house by then. But the thought of leaving this place, this neighborhood, and especially of leaving Angie, left him feeling like a hole had been dug out of his heart.

He walked outside into heavy, humid air and looked up at the cloudy sky. There was a storm coming. He could smell it.

After a short battle with himself, he looked over toward Angie's place.

His heart lifted when he caught a glimpse of red hair disappearing onto the wooded path where the kennel was.

Good, well, he hoped she liked the place, because he'd put a lot of himself into it, lots of sweet extra touches to make it cute, like what he thought a woman would enjoy.

Fat lot of good it had done him. She wasn't speaking to him, and she wanted him out.

He totally understood why. Well, not totally, but a lot.

It *was* a lot, what she'd discovered. Her husband, whom she'd thought to be a good man, had actually been cheating on her, had produced a child.

That would send anyone into a tailspin. There'd have to be a revision of her whole view of her marriage, and not in a good direction. Oscar had been a jerk, and Luke hated that the man had hurt Angie.

Was she right to be so furious at Luke, though? He'd just found out about Declan's parentage in the past couple of weeks. True, he'd decided not to tell her, but not out of ill intention.

He heard a crash and a muffled exclamation from Brian and Elizabeth's house and went over to discover Brian trying to carry a bulky rolled-up canvas toward the end of the cul-de-sac. Luke grabbed one end, and they carried it to the place Brian indicated he wanted to set it up.

"Thanks," Brian said once they'd put the bulky item down.

"Block party this weekend, and rain's predicted. You're coming, aren't you?"

Luke brushed his hands on the sides of his work pants. "Not sure. You putting this up now, or after this storm passes?"

"I'd like to get it up now," Brian said. "We need to know that it'll hold before we have a bunch of people standing under it on Saturday."

"Makes sense." Luke helped Brian lay out the tarp with the outside facing up. The wind gusted around them, the temperature getting noticeably cooler.

"You a night owl?" Brian asked as they worked together to assemble the frame. They attached the legs to it. "Saw your lights on late."

"Working on the carriage house," Luke said. "Angie wants it done by the end of the month." Her name tasted bitter in his mouth.

"You moving out then?" Brian asked.

"Looks like it."

They righted the frame and then threw the tarp over it. Working together, they pulled the tarp tight over each corner.

In the distance, thunder rumbled. Tree leaves rustled in the wind.

"I'm sorry to hear you're leaving," Brian said. "Elizabeth and I like you. You're a good addition to the neighborhood, and not just because you can give me a hand here and there."

"Never thought I'd fit in here, but I've enjoyed it," Luke said.

"You fit in fine," Brian said. "Why did you think you wouldn't?"

Luke rubbed his thumb and forefingers together. "Money. You all have it, and I don't."

Brian shrugged. "Elizabeth and I are comfortable," he said. "Seems like most of the neighbors are, too, including

Angie. But not many of us were born with a silver spoon. Keep working hard, and you'll get there."

"Maybe." Luke didn't want to share that he worried he'd never get ahead, that he'd always need to support Vanessa and Declan.

Although, to his surprise, Vanessa had seemed to be doing better the last time they'd talked. Something about getting the truth about Declan out in the open, he suspected.

Brian gave him a shrewd glance. "You know," he said, "money's not important to the man upstairs. Character is, and that, it seems to me, you've got."

"Thanks." Surprisingly, the other man's affirmation of him felt good.

He caught a glimpse of Angie leading Coco and Peppy toward the house.

She sat the dogs in front of the deck and walked a few steps away, training them. Luke could barely make out her saying, "Coco, come!" The big black dog ran to her.

Smart dog.

"Go ahead, talk to Angie," Brian said, grinning. "I've got this now."

Luke shook his head. "She's not speaking to me right at the moment."

Brian's eyebrows lifted. "A fight?"

"I messed up," Luke admitted. "She's mad enough that I don't know if it can be fixed."

Brian hammered a reinforcing stake into the ground and tied one of the tarp's strings to it. "You seem like a good guy. Did you do something that bad? Should I be kicking you out of the neighborhood?"

"I kept a secret I shouldn't have, I guess," Luke said. "It wasn't my secret to tell, but when she and I got close…" He shrugged. "Still not mine to tell, but she felt betrayed."

He was watching Angie as he spoke. She got Coco to come to her then praised the dog extravagantly.

Everything in him reached out to her, giving his chest a palpable ache.

"She'll need to talk it out, I guess." Brian tightened the line. The sky was darkening. "Either to you or other people. That's how women roll, or at least, that's how Elizabeth is and my wife before her, too."

"I guess." Luke held the tarp while Brian stretched another safety line to the stake he'd just pounded in.

"She's a great gal. Don't give up on her." Brian looked up at the sky then grabbed the last stake. "Think I'll see if I can become a therapy-dog handler once her business gets going. It's good work she does."

Lightning flashed across the sky, followed by a loud crack of thunder.

Out of the corner of his eye, Luke saw a black flash go by.

"Coco!" Angie screamed. She was holding a squirming Peppy, trying to get the smaller dog into the house.

Luke took off running after Coco as rain started falling in piercing needles. "Coco!" he yelled. He could see that the dog was trailing a leash. If he could grab that… "Coco, stay," he yelled, and the dog paused.

Another flash of lightning and boom of thunder, and Coco raced away again.

Luke had to get the dog before it ran into the busy street on the other side of the neighborhood. His arms and legs pumped, and he sucked in air as he raced after the dog.

Lightning illuminated his storm-dark surroundings. He knew another clap of thunder was coming. He dove for the leash and caught it just as the thunder boomed. Coco tried to bolt, but Luke held on. "Come on, girl, let's get you home," he said, trying to make his voice soothing, Angie-like. "This way. Come on." With gentle urging, keeping a tight grip on the leash, he made his way back toward Angie's.

In the street in front of her house, they met. "You found her!" she cried.

Luke's heart lifted as he handed her the leash. Maybe his act of semi-heroism would boost his standing with her, get her over her anger.

She knelt beside Coco, petting and praising the dog. When she looked up at Luke, his breath caught.

Her wet hair and water-slicked face were exactly like when they'd kissed. With everything in him, he wanted to pull her into his arms again.

Her eyes widened, and darkened, and he was pretty sure she was remembering their kiss, too.

A bolt of lightning flashed, farther away.

She turned away from Luke and stood. "Come on, Coco," she said, then looked back at Luke. "Thanks," she said. "Really. I appreciate what you did." She bit her lip, turned and walked away.

Leaving Luke standing in the rain, utterly confused.

Chapter Sixteen

The day after the storm, Angie decided she needed a day off from fundraising and grant writing and paperwork. But not to sit at home and brood. She needed to get out of herself and do something for somebody else.

Fortunately, her new church provided the right opportunity.

Actually, she didn't know whether she'd stick with this church or not. It was Luke's church, and she and Luke weren't on the best terms right now. But she'd liked the two services she'd attended and the people she'd met there. And she felt such a strong need for spiritual support. For God. For healing the past, like they'd prayed about the other night.

It wasn't all about her, either; it was about becoming a better person, a giving person.

And when she thought about that, about being a better person, she thought about Luke. Yes, they were at odds, but when she'd needed his help, he'd dropped everything and rushed to catch Coco before the poor pup got herself into danger during that storm. That meant something.

Gabby and Megan, too, had seemed enthusiastic about Luke. *If someone looked at me the way Luke looks at you…* Angie had to admit that she was affected by the notion. A part of her wanted to hang out with Luke a little more, just to pay attention to how he looked at her.

Of course, she'd seen his smoldering expression when they'd kissed…

But on the other hand, he was Vanessa's brother, and he'd kept Vanessa's secret—a secret Angie had every right to know.

Tired of her circling thoughts, she drove across town. A group of church members were meeting at a community garden, where people who didn't have yards or garden space could grow summer vegetables. Some of the plots had been neglected by folks who worked too much to have time to tend them, so the church members were going to help out by weeding some overgrown beds in the large field where the plots were located.

She'd heard about it from Gabby, who was in charge. Now Gabby's face lit up when she saw Angie. "You came! I'm so glad! And you brought your own tools," she added, nodding approvingly at Angie's gloves, small shovel and weed diggers. Gabby hugged her and looked at her clipboard. "I'm going to put you in plot seventeen, all the way over by the eastern edge of the field. You'll see it, the plots are all numbered."

Angie strolled over that way, waving to a few church members who already looked familiar. June sunshine beat down on her shoulders, and a breeze ruffled the surrounding trees and the vegetable plants. Birds chirped, hopping from plant to plant. A robin pulled a worm from the ground.

She was glad she'd come. This was what she needed: to get outside and help other people. To stop thinking about Oscar and his betrayal.

She saw the number seventeen on a small sign and approached the garden plot.

And stopped.

Kneeling on the ground, pulling weeds from around a row of peas, was Vanessa.

Oh, no, no, no, no. She turned around, heat rising to her face. This was the last person she wanted to see. She started walking away.

"Angie!" Vanessa's voice behind her just made her want to walk faster.

"Please, wait a minute."

If there hadn't been other people working in nearby plots who looked up to see what was going on, Angie would have kept walking. But she didn't want to appear to be a complete jerk. "What?" she asked, turning and crossing her arms.

"I asked to work with you." Standing behind her, Vanessa was out of breath, and even in her jeans and baggy shirt, Angie could see that she was bone thin. "Gabby's in charge, and I begged her to do it."

Angie closed her eyes for a brief second and shook her head. "I don't want to talk to you."

"You can change your assignment. Just give me five minutes."

Angie sucked in a breath and let it out in a sigh. Then, conscious of other church members' eyes on her, she nodded and walked back toward plot seventeen. "Five minutes."

She knelt and started pulling weeds because she couldn't stand to just sit and look at the woman who'd been with Oscar, who'd caused him to cheat. Viciously, she ripped out thistles and dandelions.

Vanessa knelt a few feet away. "Oh no, don't pull the bean plants," Vanessa said.

"I *know* what beans look like." Ugh. Vanessa was irritating on all levels.

Vanessa took the single bean plant from Angie's little

pile of weeds and tucked it back into the ground, tapping the earth around it. "I didn't know he was married," she said to the dirt in front of her.

Angie sat back on her heels and stared at the woman. The audacity! "You expect me to believe that?"

Vanessa glanced over at her and shrugged. "No, I'm sure you don't." She started pulling weeds from the next row. "We met when he was on business in Philadelphia. I was there partying with friends. That was my lifestyle then. We liked to go to the nice hotels where rich businessmen would buy us drinks."

"When was this?" Angie asked, her eyes narrowing.

Vanessa named the month and year, corresponding to the holiday season before the time Angie determined that Declan was conceived. Reluctantly, she remembered a Philadelphia business trip that had gone on longer than planned, causing Oscar to miss several holiday parties. In fact, he'd only come home on Christmas Eve.

He'd brought Angie a gorgeous diamond necklace, and he'd been so sweet with his apologies that she'd forgiven him. She still cherished the necklace...or at least, she had.

No more.

Vanessa went on with her explanation. "We met in the hotel bar, and I don't want to blame him like he seduced me or forced me to be with him. I was a responsible adult, or I should have been. But I was immature. I wasn't a Christian then, and I didn't know what to look for in a man nor how I should behave when I met someone."

"Did you know to look for a wedding ring?" Angie couldn't keep the bitterness out of her voice.

Vanessa met her eyes. "I did look. He wasn't wearing one."

Angie hated the picture Vanessa was painting. She'd known Oscar went out with business associates when he was on his trips, and of course, women would find him attractive. He had been distinguished in his custom business suits, charming and sophisticated. Quick to pick up a tab. Always carrying wads of cash.

She focused on the weeds in front of her, yanking them out.

"Can I tell you more?" Vanessa sat, arms around knees.

There was more? But of course there was; there was Declan. She shrugged and kept weeding.

"We, uh, stayed involved after Philly since we were both from here. Or I shouldn't say involved. We met up a few times, but when we were both sober, he didn't look so good to me. Nor I to him, probably. He wouldn't let me call him, and he didn't want to go out. We could only meet at my place because, he said, his was under construction."

"We had some renovations going on," Angie said. "Guess he knew that when you lie, it's best to stick close to the truth."

"Right." Vanessa let out a bitter chuckle. "I started doing research and found out who he was. When I realized he was married, I broke it off."

"Uh-huh." She knew her doubt was obvious in her voice.

From the corner of her eye, Angie saw Vanessa reach toward her as if to touch her arm. She pulled it away.

"Then." Vanessa cleared her throat. "Then, I found out I was pregnant."

Angie stared at the dirt and plants in front of her until the green and brown blurred together. Angrily she backhanded tears away. "I don't believe any of this," she choked out.

"I'm not surprised." Vanessa scooted over on her knees and pulled one weed then another. "I just wanted you to know. You seem like a good person, and I wouldn't have done it to you if I'd known."

Angie snorted and didn't say *Yeah, right*. She just thought it.

"Also," Vanessa said, her voice suddenly sharp and intense, "I need you not to take your feelings out on Declan."

Angie looked up quickly. "I wouldn't."

They were silent for a few minutes. A red-winged blackbird sang from the tall grasses that adjoined the garden area.

Angie thought about everything she'd just heard. She didn't want to believe it, but she was starting to. There were too many pieces that fit together.

"Declan knew who Oscar was. In the picture." She swallowed hard and looked at Vanessa. "How did he know?"

Vanessa nodded. "Yes. Oscar came to visit periodically, and he always brought gifts. Gifts for Declan, and money to help us out. Once Declan was old enough to want that, he looked forward to the gifts and the way we could have a few more luxuries after Oscar had come by."

Angie huffed out a breath. "Nice for you," she muttered.

"Luxuries like hamburgers instead of boxed mac and cheese, Angie. I'm pretty sure he didn't take food off your table."

Those quiet words ripped Angie out of her own perspective, and she suddenly pictured what it must have been like for Vanessa. Having a child out of wedlock, learning the father was married, having him come by only occasionally and only to bring a little grocery money and a few gifts.

The fact remained that Vanessa had a child and Angie didn't. Oscar had said he didn't want children. "What was his attitude toward Declan?"

"He was proud Declan was a boy. But he didn't really know how to handle kids, so if Declan cried, he was outta there." Vanessa sighed and looked off toward the horizon. "His visits got less frequent and finally petered out. He got busy with other things, I guess." She shook her head. "To tell the truth, I was just as glad. There was nothing between us, and it was getting awkward answering Declan's questions."

"I'm sure," Angie said. At least Declan had known to ask questions. Angie hadn't. She'd been such a fool.

"When I realized the relationship was completely over, I asked him to help me out financially with Declan, to give me money on a regular basis. So...he bought me a house. It's not much, but it's been a place to raise Declan. He made the payments on it and gave us a little money besides, on the condition that I kept it all quiet." She looked over at Angie. "I'm sorry. That money should have been yours."

"Money's not what bothers me. I'm fine. I'm glad..." She swallowed hard. "I'm glad he helped you. But I guess that stopped when he passed away."

"Well...that's complicated. His executor—Josiah Harmon, do you know him? He's a lawyer."

"Oh, I know Josiah." Josiah had been remarkably slow about working through Oscar's will.

"Bit of a jerk," Vanessa said matter-of-factly. "But he came to me and explained how Oscar had set it up. Apparently, he left money to Josiah to dole out to me. But Josiah was to keep an eye on me. If I ever started telling people who Declan's dad was, the money would stop."

Angie took off her gloves and let her face fall into her hands, shaking her head at the same time. "Unbelievable."

A couple from the church came by and offered to help them finish their section, but both Angie and Vanessa waved them away. "We'd better work on this while we talk," Angie said, and they both started pulling weeds with renewed vigor.

"So," Vanessa continued. "I told Luke not even three weeks ago, when I knew he was having feelings for you. But I explained how my finances depended on him keeping it to himself."

Angie had stiffened at the mention of Luke's name. "So that's why he lied to me, you're saying?"

"Yes. I guess. If he even lied." She paused in her work. "Whatever you feel about me, don't blame Luke. He's been taking care of me since we were kids in foster care. Sees it as his job, since our parents had too many problems to do it. He's a protector to the core, Angie. It's who he is. It's what he does."

Angie drew in a breath and let it out, slowly. She couldn't be surprised that Luke had chosen his sister over her, but it still hurt. He'd spent multiple hours with her and Declan, all the while knowing that the boy's father was Angie's husband.

And yes, maybe he'd done it because he was a protector to the core, like Vanessa had said. When would someone prioritize Angie enough to protect her, though?

Maybe he thinks you're strong enough to handle things. Unlike Oscar, who'd rescued her from her former life and then always thought of her as just a little less than him, less than other friends and acquaintances who hadn't degraded themselves to survive.

Angie put that thought aside to explore later. She couldn't deal with changing her view of Luke, not right now. "How's Declan handling things? Does he understand?"

"No. He's too young." Vanessa tossed a weed into her nearly full bushel basket. "I told him there were some complicated grown-up things going on, that was why you had Oscar's picture, but the important thing was that his dad loved him."

Slowly, Angie nodded.

"I'd truly appreciate it if you'd stick to that story and not spread any negativity you feel onto Declan."

"Of course." She didn't want to hurt Declan. None of this was his fault.

"I don't know if it helps, but Oscar wasn't faithful to me, either. Even during the couple of months I was seeing him, he went out with one of my friends."

"What?" Angie stared. "There were more women?" She wrapped her arms around herself and rocked back and forth. "How did I not know any of this?"

"I only know about one," Vanessa said quickly. "And the only way I knew was that she told me. He was...well, I guess you know he was great in some ways. Charming and convincing." She hesitated. "My friend and I, we figured out that he liked girls with rough backgrounds. He liked to kind of save them. Only, obviously not you."

Angie's head was spinning. "It was me, too. That was why he liked me, too." She didn't elaborate, and after looking at her for a moment, Vanessa nodded and didn't ask questions.

They weeded the rest of the plot in silence, aside from the sound of the birds and the voices of a few other gardeners on the other side of the field. As they walked back with their baskets of weeds, Vanessa said, "Thank you. Thank you for listening."

"Thank you for telling me." It wasn't like she wanted to be friends with Vanessa, but she did admire her courage in telling the truth.

"And I'm fine with giving up the financial benefit. I'm not going to hide because of Josiah Harmon. I'm not going to hide at all anymore because...well, I'm sorry because I know all this information hurt you, but I feel like a weight's lifted."

"I'm sure you do."

"And Angie, give Luke a chance. He was stuck in a dilemma. He couldn't tell you—"

"Stop," Angie said. "I just can't deal with more right now."

"Of course. I understand."

There wasn't anything Angie could do to change the past.

But there was one thing she could do, and soon. "I'm going to give Josiah Harmon a call," she said. "I think I, or we, should pay him a visit."

"Really?" Vanessa stared at her. "You'd do that now? Report me to him so he stops—"

"No, no." She squeezed Vanessa's arm, ever so briefly. "I want to talk to him about doing the right thing by you and by Declan. Which means paying a reasonable amount of child support out of the money Oscar designated for it, and if there's not enough there, well... I inherited enough from Oscar to keep up that commitment until Declan comes of age."

Vanessa's mouth opened into a wide O. "You're joking."

"Nope." She dumped her basket of weeds. "I'm obviously not happy that Oscar cheated on me. And honestly, I'm jealous that you got to have a child and I didn't. But none of this is Declan's fault. He had a wealthy father, and he should benefit from that. He, and you, shouldn't live in poverty."

Vanessa threw her arms around Angie and then pulled back. "Sorry. It's just, you're an amazing woman. No matter whether we can work it out with Josiah or not, I just think... oh, wow. Just thank you." She hugged her again.

Angie let Vanessa hug her, this woman who'd had an affair with Angie's husband, although apparently without knowing he was a married man. Then she walked back to her car, musing on the day.

She'd intended to get out of herself and do good for others by weeding a garden. She'd ended up doing good, maybe, for another woman and child who needed help. She hadn't exactly gotten out of herself, but she'd gotten out of her self-centered emotions of hurt.

As she drove home, she realized she was feeling better about herself.

How she felt about Luke…well, that was still an open question.

She thought about it most of that evening, while she worked with Coco and made pasta salad and cookies for the block party.

Would she have wanted Luke to instantly let her know Declan's parentage the moment he'd found out about it?

Sure, there were people who rushed to share bad news, enjoying the drama of other people's problems. Luke wasn't that kind of person. He was the opposite. He was a quiet man who tried to help other people as best he could.

He'd been trying to help Vanessa financially, and he hadn't wanted to jeopardize the stipend she was getting from Oscar's executor. A stipend that, upon texting Vanessa to ask for clarification on the monthly amount, she learned was way too low. Angie knew it because she'd listened to some of Oscar's friends bemoan the high amount of child support they'd had to send to their ex-wives.

There wasn't much she could make right in the whole situation, but a reasonable level of child support was one thing she could provide. First, though, she was going to meet with Josiah next week and confront him with some cold, hard facts.

And then she'd think about whether she and Luke could salvage anything out of this whole difficult situation. If he even still wanted to.

Chapter Seventeen

Luke attended the block party on Saturday afternoon with mixed feelings. He'd grown fond of the neighborhood and of the people he'd met there, especially Brian and Elizabeth. In fact, everyone was friendly: talking, laughing, making summer plans.

For Luke, it felt like goodbye.

It was a perfect June day, blue sky, temperature in the seventies, no humidity to speak of. He was helping one of the neighbors carry a big ice chest to the drink area when he saw Vanessa and Declan walk into the party area.

What on earth were they thinking?

Luke had low expectations for the day, but he did hope to have a cordial, friendly word with Angie. She'd seemed to soften a little since he'd rescued Coco from the storm and had even waved hello to him this morning.

Still, having Vanessa and Declan here would rub salt in wounds that were obviously still raw.

He set the ice chest down in the drink area and then strode over to his sister and nephew. "Are you sure this is a good idea?" he asked Vanessa quietly.

Vanessa hugged him. "I've got this," she said, also quiet so Declan couldn't hear. "I fixed my end of it."

As Declan ran off toward Brian and Elizabeth's grandkids, Luke gestured Vanessa to a picnic bench. "How's Declan handing it all? And what do you mean, you fixed it?"

"I talked to Angie," she said calmly. "I explained the situation, and while I'm not gonna say she's fine with it, she accepts it."

"Wow." He had to hand it to Angie, if what Vanessa said was true. To both of them, really.

"As for Declan, he's doing fine. He's a kid, focused on kid things like he should be." She straightened. "But, Luke, we need to talk about something. I know you've been working hard to earn enough for me to go to that residential program, but I don't want to take all your money. And I don't want to leave Declan for six or eight weeks. I talked to Gabby, Declan's teacher, and she helped me find free counseling and an eating disorder program for older women. It's not residential, it's live video group sessions. I'm already starting it."

He stared at his sister. He often thought of her as younger than she was, needy, suffering. But she didn't seem that way now. "How expensive?" he asked.

"That's the other thing. Angie spoke with the executor of Oscar's will and also to a lawyer she knows. One way or another, she's going to make sure that I get real child support for Declan. Even to the point of paying it out herself if need be."

Luke's jaw about dropped. He looked over at Angie, intuitively aware of where she was at all times. "She said she'd do that?"

"Yes, and I believe her. She's a good woman, Luke. A really good woman."

She was, and Luke had known it, but this was above and beyond.

"Try to make it work with her," Vanessa urged. "You're a great brother, and you've taken care of me since forever, but I need to stand on my own two feet. And if you and she have found love together, you need to grab it." She hugged him, and when he held her away to look into her face, to make sure she meant it, he detected a slightly wistful expression. As if maybe, one day, Vanessa might like to find love for herself.

"How'd you grow up so much, all of a sudden?" he asked.

She lifted her hands, palms up. "I guess the jolt of it all coming out. Holding that secret inside for all those years, that was bringing me down." She smiled at him. "I've done some praying, and I've gotten help from friends. And confessing the truth to Angie was healing."

"I'm glad for you," he said, his throat a little bit tight. "Glad for Declan, too. You're going to do just fine."

"I am." Vanessa stood. "And I'm going to go mingle. You should work things out with Angie. Don't be a martyr for my sake, Luke. You don't have to do that anymore."

Before he could respond to that, his sister was gone.

He wandered through the party, talking to people, helping where he was needed, his head spinning from his conversation with Vanessa.

He looked over to Angie again and was inspired by his sister. If Vanessa had had the guts to talk to her, he could, too.

He was also motivated by a couple of guys that seemed overly interested in her, one of them at least ten years too young.

It might be too late, and it might not work, but he was going to try. This time, he was choosing love over fear.

He had no grand gesture to make. He just approached her, his heart pounding.

She turned away from the too young guy and watched Luke approach.

"Want to take a walk?" Luke asked.

She lifted an eyebrow, then turned to the guy who still stood beside her. "Excuse me," she said. "It was nice meeting you." Then she took Luke's arm. They walked a few steps and stopped. "Were you just trying to save me from that silly young man, or do you really want to take a walk?"

"Take a walk," he said. "I want to talk to you."

"Well," she said, "I do need to walk Coco and Peppy." But as she got the dogs and leashed them up, Caleb and Declan came running. "Can we walk them?" Declan asked.

Luke watched to see Angie's reaction to Declan. It seemed the same as always. No, not quite. She was studying Declan with a little curiosity, a little sadness. "Keep a good grip on them," she instructed the boys. "Put your hand through the loop and hold the leash. Like this." She demonstrated and watched both boys do as she'd said.

As they rushed off with the excited dogs, she looked up at him. "Where to?"

He wished they were on a street in Paris or walking under a waterfall at a Caribbean resort. But they were only here, on a residential street in Chesapeake Corners, Maryland. It would have to do.

"This way," he said, and they strolled toward the quiet part of the street.

He needed to speak before he lost his nerve. "Look," he said, "I'm sure you're raw from all that's happened. I just want to apologize."

"It's not needed," she said, to his surprise. "I understand from talking to Vanessa that you were in an impossible situation."

He couldn't believe she'd accepted his apology so quickly. But he had to clarify. "I was," he said. "I didn't know the truth about Declan yet when I started having feelings for you, but I did know Vanessa had been involved with your husband. In that situation, I had no right to kiss you. I apologize for that and for any mixed messages I gave you."

She smiled a little. "You did give mixed messages," she said. "And I guess… I accept your apology for kissing me, too." She looked at him inquiringly, as if to say, is that all?

It wasn't. "I apologize for kissing you," he said, "but I'm not sorry for it."

"Really?"

"I couldn't have kept my distance if I'd tried," he said. "Because…" He hesitated, shot up a quick prayer and went for it. "Because I want to do it again."

She stared at him and then looked over his shoulder at the small crowd enjoying the block party. "I don't think—"

"Not now," he said quickly. "But someday. And more than once. Angie…is there any chance you'd go out with me? In spite of everything that's happened?"

Her pretty green eyes widened. "I… I don't know what to say."

That wasn't promising, but Luke wasn't going to give up so easily. "I appreciate your warmth and caring. You're so good to people, and you care so much about kids. You're gorgeous, of course, but you're not stuck-up about it. You're fun. And you've managed to grow in faith despite some big challenges."

Her eyes looked a little shiny, as if she were holding back tears. "You shouldn't fall in love with me," she said. "You're a good Christian man, and I'm a former exotic dancer."

He took her hand, and she let him. "You're way more than that," he said. "You're a wonderful woman with so much depth because you've been through a lot and came out on the other side. Your past made you you, just like my past made me me." He paused. "I heard about what you're going to do for Vanessa. That just shows me what I'd already come to realize. You're incredibly generous, and you have a forgiving heart. You're the kind of woman I want to…"

He stopped himself in time. He knew what he wanted—he'd known it for a while—and although he could see a possibility of making it permanent with Angie, he didn't want to ruin it by declaring himself too soon. "You're the kind of woman I want to spend more time with. Explore what we might have together."

She bit her lip. "Is it because you want to save me?" she asked.

He tilted his head to one side, surprised. "Save you? If anything, I'm the one who needs saving."

"From what?" she asked.

"From loneliness. From a life where I don't trust anyone. From being focused on myself."

She looked up at him, and tears rolled down her cheeks now.

"Am I making you happy or sad?" he asked, suddenly insecure.

She laughed a little and squeezed his hand. "Happy," she said. "Luke, I care for you, too. You're so strong and kind. And you're *not* focused on yourself. You help everyone. I feel like I can learn from you and grow with you."

His heart felt like it was about to burst, but his innate caution held him back. "There's a lot to overcome," he said, "with Declan being who he is."

They both looked over to a big fenced yard where Declan and Caleb were playing with the dogs. She sighed, looking sad.

Which made sense. "Can you handle being around me and Declan—and Vanessa—after how you've been hurt? If friends is all we can be, then I'll take that."

She looked up at him, an eyebrow raised, her eyes sparkling through her tears. "Maybe more than friends," she said. "If you'd be interested."

He couldn't help it then. He turned and faced her and

pulled her into his arms. "I want way more than friendship," he said. "I want…" He wanted this woman at his side for the rest of his life, but it wasn't time to say that, not yet. Instead, he just kissed her.

And got a little lost, until he heard something behind him. He lifted his head and looked.

Declan and Caleb stood at the gate, making gagging sounds and laughing. "Uncle Luke! You're not supposed to kiss Miss Angie!"

"Well, he can if she's his girlfriend," Caleb said. He opened the gate and swung on it. "My mom was someone's girlfriend once, and she kissed him."

Declan wrinkled his nose. "I saw Brandon Jones kiss Sara Wanamaker on the playground," he said. "But she ran away and told the teacher, and he had to have in-school suspension."

Luke just stood there with his arm around Angie, both of them laughing. And then Angie knelt down and pulled Luke to his knees beside her and clicked her tongue for Peppy and Coco to come to them. The dogs didn't need a second invitation. They rushed forward into Angie's lap.

"Come on, boys," she said. "You're definitely too young to think about kissing girls, but these pups would like to give *you* kisses."

The boys dove toward them. As they laughed and groaned and got messy dog kisses, Luke looked at the woman beside him with something like awe.

She was gorgeous and forgiving, fun and kind. And she'd agreed to go out with *him*.

He lifted his face to the blue summer sky and thanked God for the blessing of it all.

Epilogue

Four months later

Fall sunshine shone on the official grand opening of the therapy-dog program. When Angie had realized she needed more space, Brian and Elizabeth had gladly sold her some of their land to grow the program. The additional kennels Luke had built were fabulous, and so were the runs, and there was plenty of room for everyone to gather in the backyard.

Vanessa was there, looking healthy and pink cheeked. Declan was at his mother's side, but only briefly; he was running around with other kids. There were Megan and Gabby, Angie's firm friends now. Plenty of dogs, too. And was that...

"What's Rambo doing here?" she asked Vanessa, amazed. She'd visited the cute dog each time she'd gone to the shelter, but she hadn't felt it right to take him away from a family.

"Caleb adopted him!" Declan explained. "We would've, but Mom's going to get a service dog."

"Maybe," Vanessa said, squeezing Declan's shoulder. "Meanwhile, Declan's helping Caleb train Rambo."

Luke, who always seemed to be close by these days, walked over. They'd spent so much time together learning and growing, building their relationship. They were steady, exclusive boyfriend and girlfriend now, and it was more than Angie had ever hoped for. "Everything going okay?" he asked.

"It's going great." She leaned against him briefly.

Angie noticed people looking at someone walking down the driveway to her house. She was young, with long blond hair flowing down her back and a tight shirt and jeans.

Angie waved. "Nicki!" she called.

The other woman came over and hugged her. A boy about Declan's age was at her side. Angie knelt in front of the child. "How's the reading going?" she asked.

"Better when I read to the dog!" the child said then looked up at Nicki. "Can I go play with the kids, Mom?"

"Yes, but stay close."

He ran off to play, and Angie walked around introducing the woman to others at the event. She'd visited her old workplace a few times and talked to the dancers. They were all different from when she'd been there, of course—exotic dancing was a young women's game—but they had similar problems. Several weren't good readers and had dropped out of school. Angie was helping them get into literacy classes. When she'd learned that Nicki had a son who struggled with reading in school, she'd gotten the boy into her dog reading program.

Someone tapped her shoulder. "Time to start."

Angie took a deep breath, climbed the steps to the make-shift stage and thanked everyone for being there. "We have a demonstration," she said and gestured Caleb to the stage.

He trotted up confidently, Peppy at his side. "Watch what reading to dogs can do," she said and stepped to the side of the stage.

Caleb sat down and read to Peppy a whole page without an error. "See, I can read good now!" he crowed, and everyone laughed and clapped.

"Caleb is at grade level in reading now," Angie explained,

"thanks in part to Peppy's first-rate work." She picked the dog up, and people cheered.

Off to the side, she saw Mrs. Ralston-Jones bending over a table in the donation area. Could she possibly be writing a check?

Angie walked off the stage and accepted all the congratulations, but her eyes kept returning to Luke. He stood to the side, letting her have her moment, watching and smiling.

Their connection felt like electricity. When he beckoned to her, she excused herself from the onlookers, left Peppy playing with a couple of other dogs and walked over.

"Great job up there," he said, hugging her. "Do you have a minute to talk?"

"Of course." She kissed his cheek.

He took her hand and led her to a small stone bench underneath a maple, its leaves flaming orange. He knelt and pulled a small box out of his pocket, and Angie gasped, her hands flying to her mouth.

He looked up at her with that smile that always melted her. "I love you," he said. "I don't have all the pretty words, but… I fell in love with you before we ever kissed, and I've only come to love you more in the past few months we've been dating. You're such a kind, fun, beautiful woman, and you make me want to be a better man, a family man, and… Angie, will you marry me?"

Joy made her heart so full she couldn't speak. Declan crept up behind Luke, and he was…oh. He was taking pictures with someone's phone.

Luke waved him away. "She didn't answer yet!"

But Angie laughed and pulled Luke to the bench beside her and kissed him, long and lingering. "Is that enough of an answer?" she asked.

He shook his head. "I want to hear you say it. I don't think I can believe you until you do."

She took his hand and kissed it. "I do want to marry you. I want to spend the rest of my life with you. Maybe even adopt some kids together. Definitely, lots of dogs. But mostly, I just want to be with the best man I know. You make me a better woman, Luke Johnson, and I want to keep growing with you. So…yes." She looked behind him at Declan and raised her voice. "Yes, yes, yes!"

"Yay!" Declan danced around, leading the applause of a small but enthusiastic audience. Cameras recorded the moment, but Angie couldn't stop looking at Luke. Couldn't believe her life had come to such a wonderful place with a wonderful man.

"I'm sorry," Luke said. "Declan was supposed to keep it quiet and just take a few pictures, but it looks like he's no good at keeping secrets." He wrapped his arms around her. "I can't be mad, though. You said yes!"

"I'm not mad about a single thing, either." In fact, she wanted to shout the news from the rooftops.

"Where's the ring?" someone called.

Only now did Luke open the black velvet box he'd been holding. He slipped a simple diamond ring onto her finger, and she knew him well enough to detect a hint of insecurity in his eyes. He'd seen the ring from her previous marriage; it had been huge, visible in a few old pictures she still had in the house.

And she'd hated the ostentation of it, the attention it had drawn. The pretty, tasteful ring Luke had chosen was exactly right. She looked into Luke's eyes. "This is perfect," she said. "You're perfect. I can't wait to spend my future with you."

* * * * *

*If you enjoyed this K9 Companions book,
don't miss* His New Companion *by Jill Kemerer,
available next month!*

*And watch for Lee Tobin McClain's
next K9 Companions book coming in
September 2025 from Love Inspired!*

Dear Reader,

Thank you for reading Luke and Angie's story! Or should I say, Luke and Angie and Peppy's story...

I first learned about literacy programs featuring dogs when my daughter was small. We visited a public library often, and one day, a dog was there to listen to children read. The minute I saw how eagerly the kids awaited their turn, I realized the brilliance of using therapy dogs to help children enjoy books and reading.

Luke and Angie are very different people on the surface. She's a wealthy widow, and he's a struggling handyman. She spent time on cruises while he was at war. But it turns out that they have more in common than they ever expected, including serious past challenges to overcome. They're also both the victims of other people's secrets.

At times, both of them think their problems are way too big to be resolved. It takes friends, faith and a cute Cavalier King Charles spaniel to bring these two people right where they belong—together.

Look for future stories set in Chesapeake Corners. I think Gabby deserves her own book, don't you? And keep watching for Vanessa's story, too!

All my best,
Lee